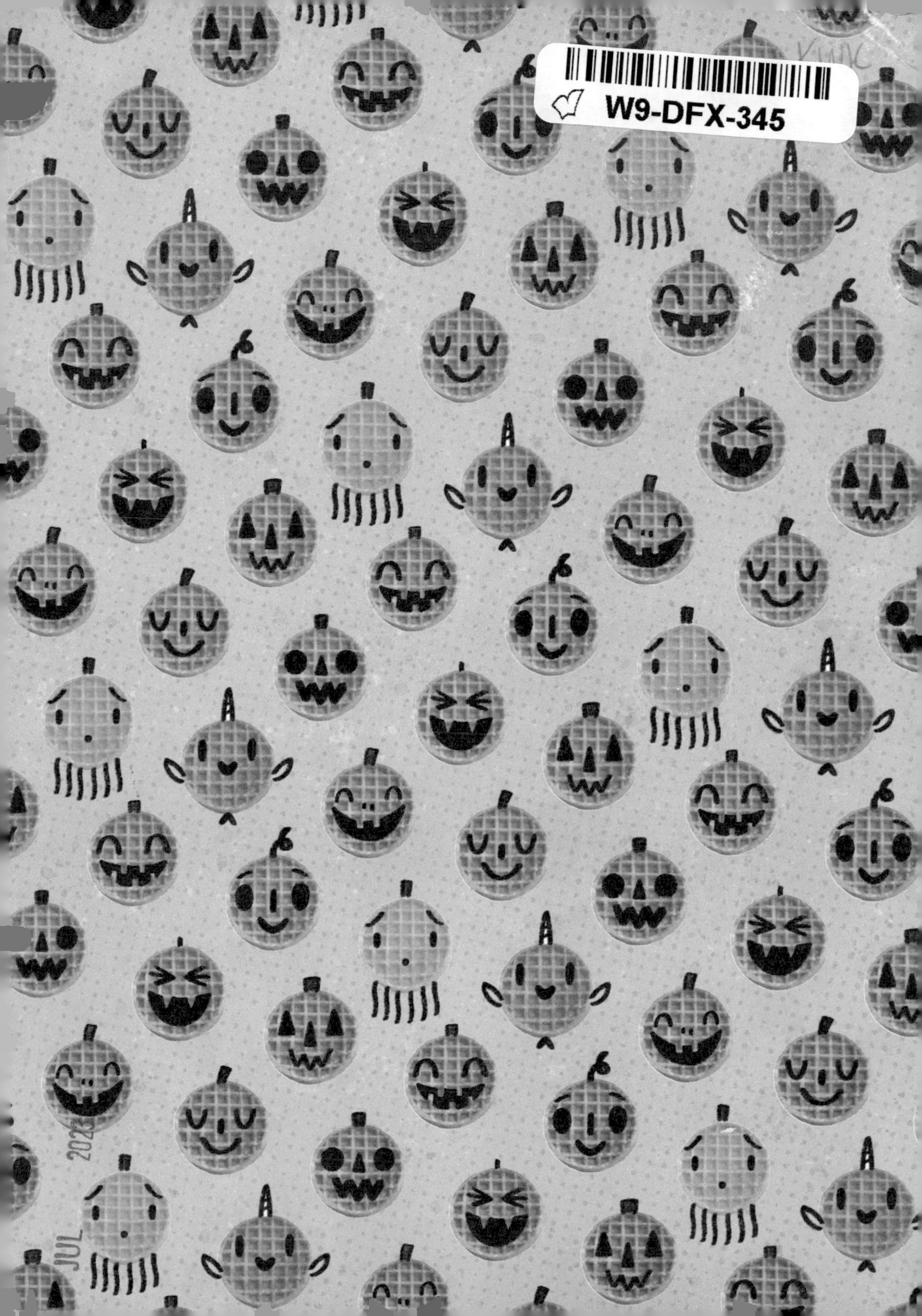

HAVE YOU READ THESE
NARWHAL AND JELLY BOOKS?

NARWHAL: UNICORN OF THE SEA!

SUPER NARWHAL AND JELLY JOLT

PEANUT BUTTER AND JELLY

NARWHAL'S OTTER FRIEND

HAPPY NARWHALIDAYS

NARWHAL'S SCHOOL OF AWESOMENESS

NARWHALICORN AND JELLY

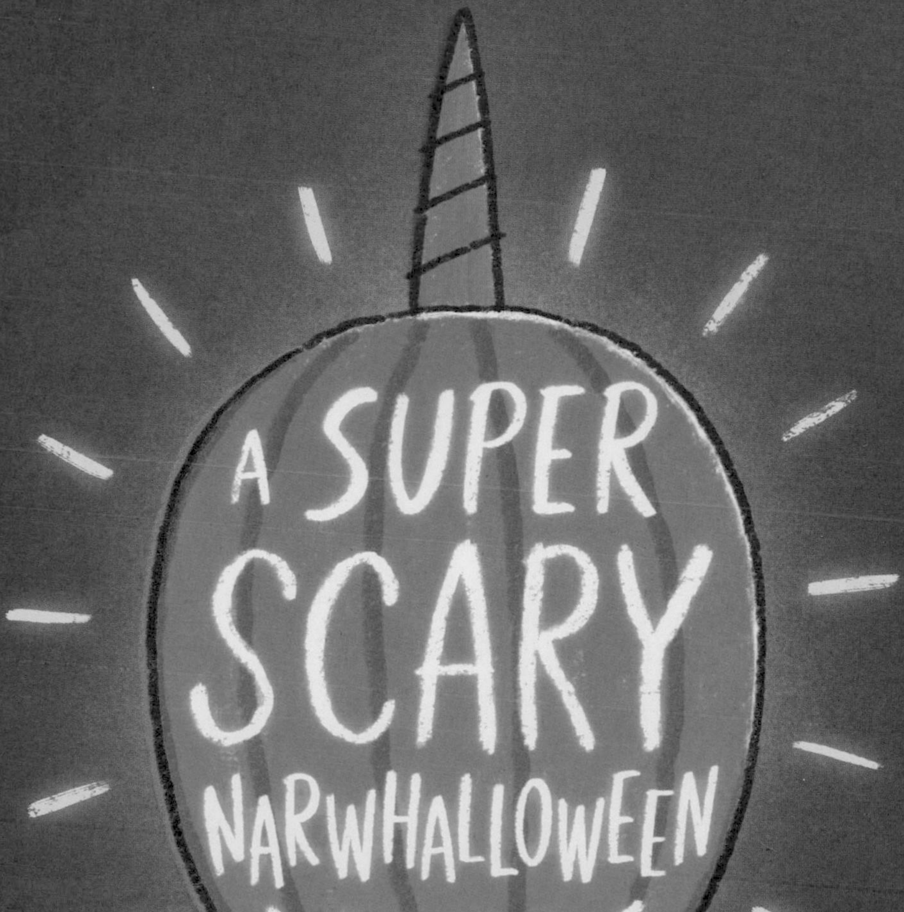
A SUPER
SCARY
NARWHALLOWEEN

BEN CLANTON

tundra

FOR THE SCARY AWESOME ANDY!

Text and illustrations copyright © 2023 by Ben Clanton

Tundra Books, an imprint of Tundra Book Group,
a division of Penguin Random House of Canada Limited

Library and Archives Canada Cataloguing in Publication

Title: A super scary Narwhalloween / Ben Clanton.
Names: Clanton, Ben, 1988- author, artist.
Series: Clanton, Ben, 1988- Narwhal and Jelly book ; 8.
Description: Series statement: A Narwhal and Jelly book ; 8
Identifiers: Canadiana (print) 20220269718 | Canadiana (ebook) 20220269785 |
ISBN 9780735266742 (hardcover) | ISBN 9780735266759 (EPUB) |
ISBN 9781774883761 (special markets)
Subjects: LCGFT: Comics (Graphic works) | LCGFT: Graphic novels.
Classification: LCC PZ7.7.C53 Sus 2023 | DDC j741.5/973—dc23

Published simultaneously in the United States of America by Tundra Books of Northern New York, an imprint of Tundra Book Group, a division of Penguin Random House of Canada Limited

Library of Congress Control Number: 2022940738

Edited by Tara Walker and Peter Phillips
Designed by Ben Clanton
The artwork in this book was rendered using mainly Procreate and Adobe Photoshop.
The text was set in a typeface based on hand-lettering by Ben Clanton.

Photos: (pumpkin) © topseller/Shutterstock; (strawberry) © Valentina Razumova/ Shutterstock; (waffle) © Tiger Images/Shutterstock; (apple) © ffolas/Shutterstock; (pear) © Nataliya Schmidt/Shutterstock; (banana) © Ian 2010/Shutterstock; (boom box) © valio84sl/Thinkstock

Printed in China

www.penguinrandomhouse.ca

1   2   3   4   5   27   26   25   24   23

tundra | Penguin Random House
TUNDRA BOOKS

CONTENTS

(5) BAMBOOZLED: A COSTUME CONUNDRUM

(23) FANGTASTIC FACTS

(25) THE GREAT GURGLE

(45) SUPER WAFFLE, STRAWBERRY SIDEKICK AND THE BAT ATTACK

(50) A BIT ABOUT BATS

(51) JELLY JOLT AND THE MONSTROUS MESS!

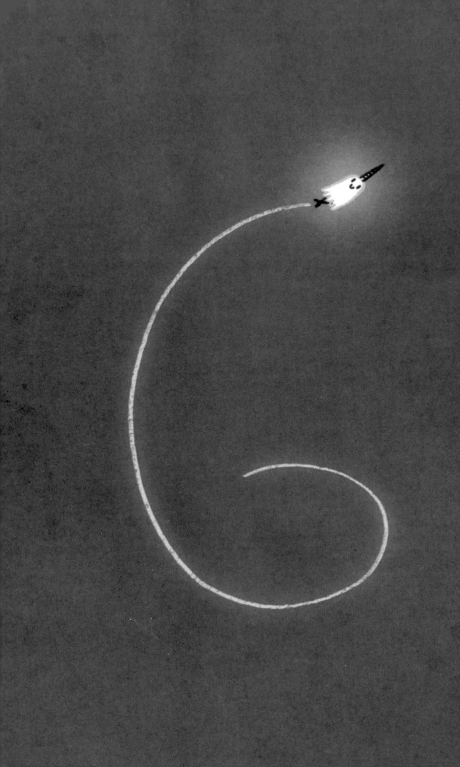

BAM**BOO**zLED

A COSTUME
CONUNDRUM

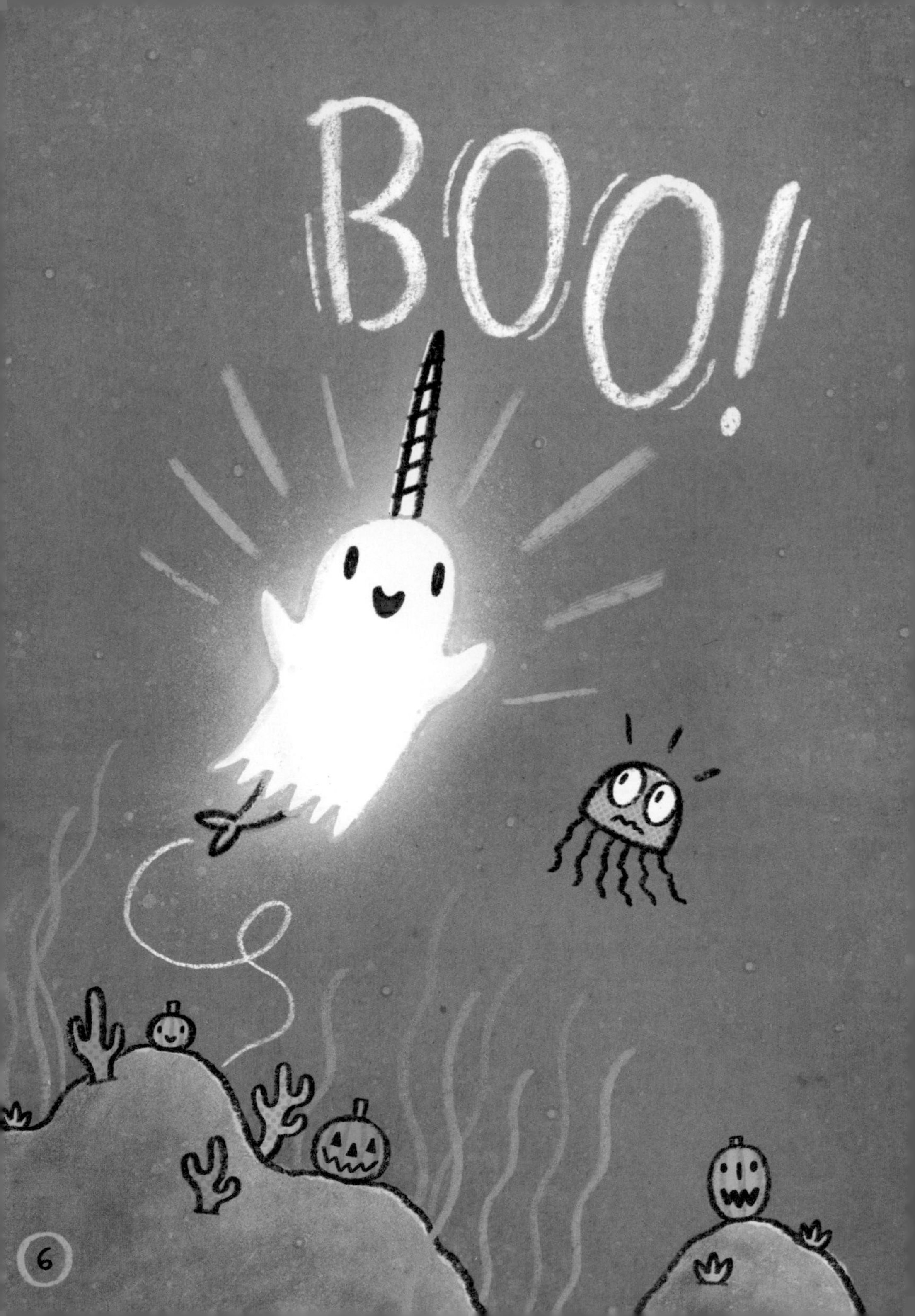
BOO!

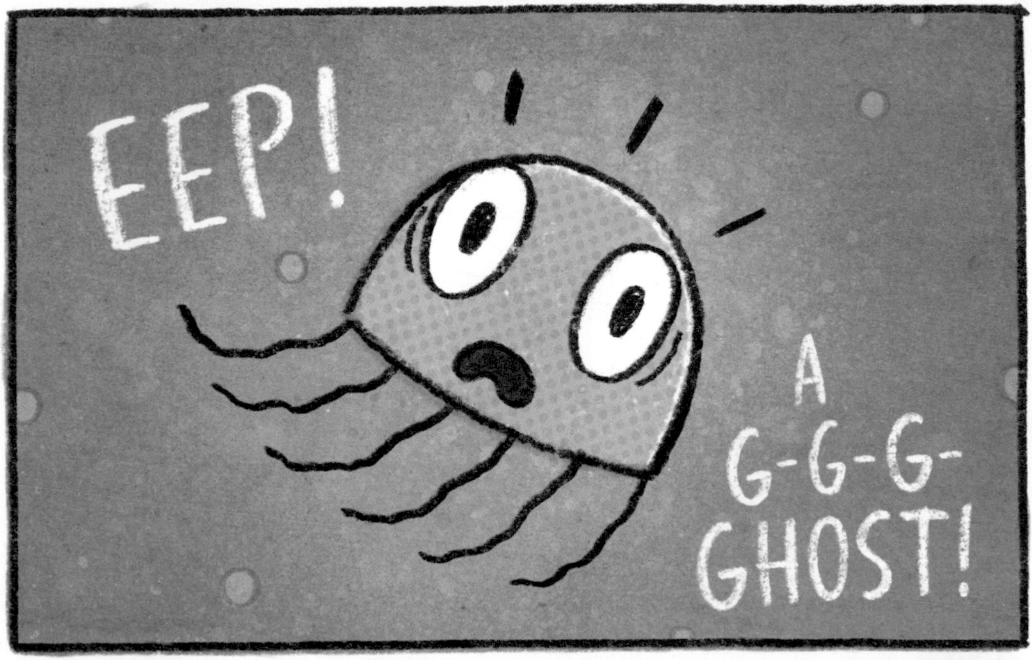
EEP!
A G-G-G-GHOST!

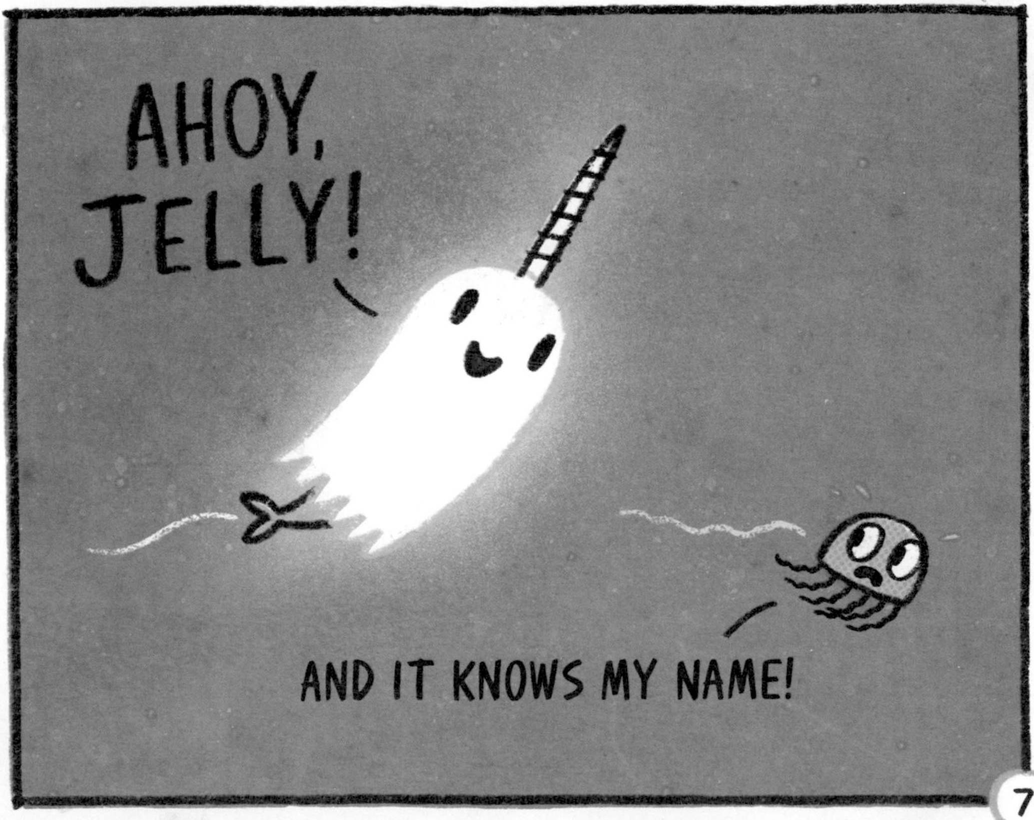
AHOY, JELLY!
AND IT KNOWS MY NAME!

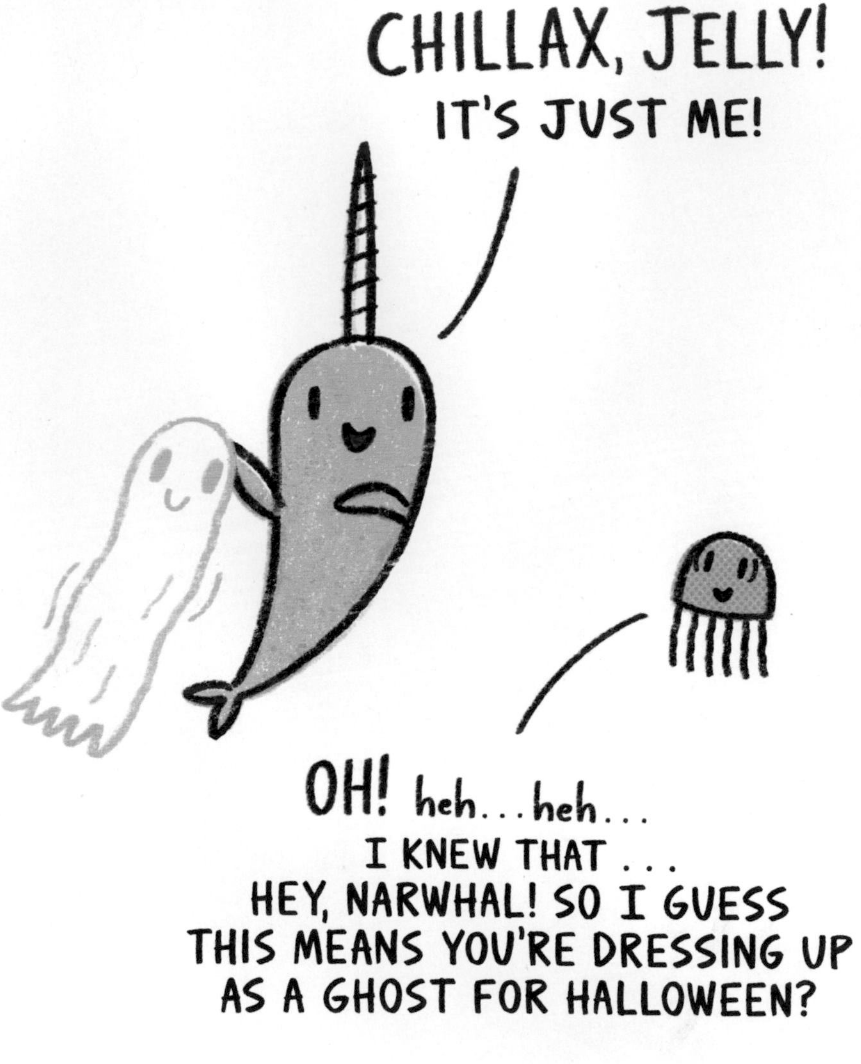
CHILLAX, JELLY!
IT'S JUST ME!
OH! heh...heh...
I KNEW THAT ...
HEY, NARWHAL! SO I GUESS
THIS MEANS YOU'RE DRESSING UP
AS A GHOST FOR HALLOWEEN?

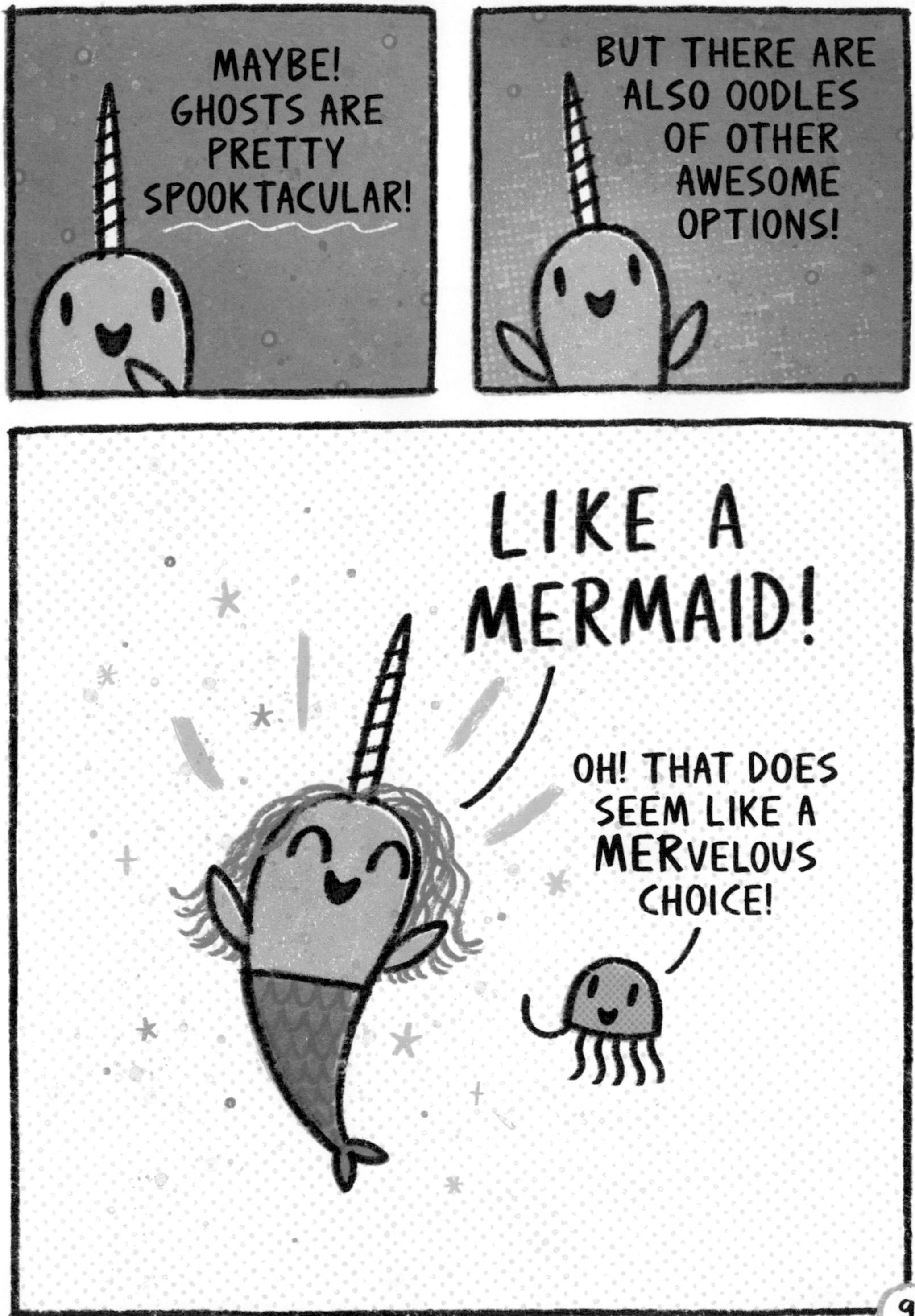
MAYBE! GHOSTS ARE PRETTY SPOOKTACULAR!
BUT THERE ARE ALSO OODLES OF OTHER AWESOME OPTIONS!
LIKE A MERMAID!
OH! THAT DOES SEEM LIKE A MERVELOUS CHOICE!

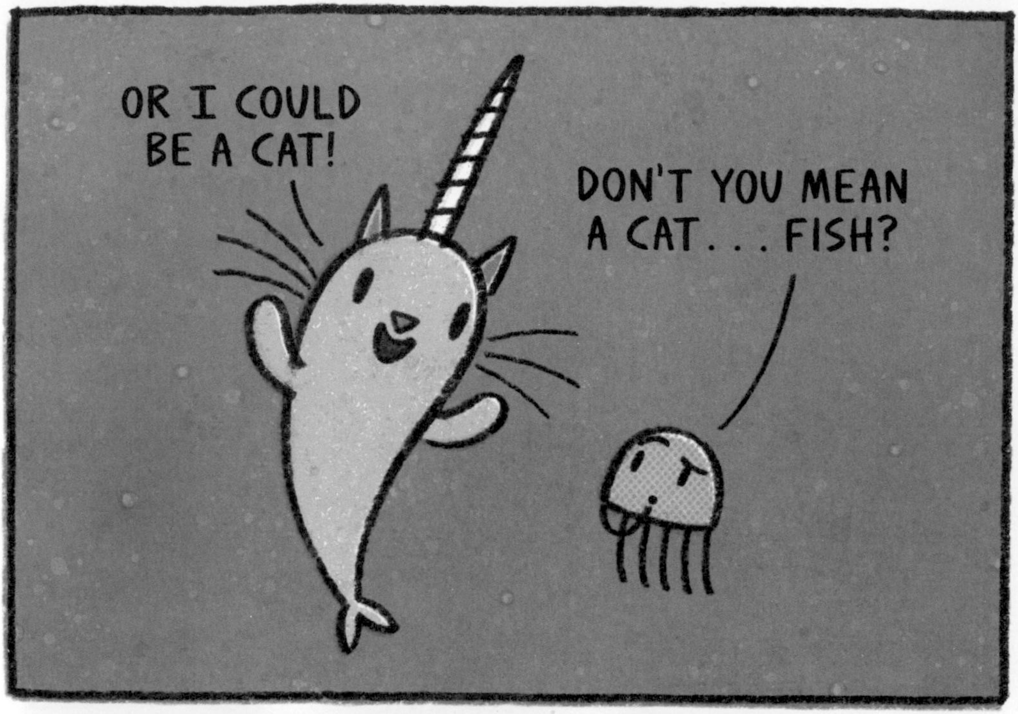
OR I COULD BE A CAT!
DON'T YOU MEAN A CAT. . . FISH?

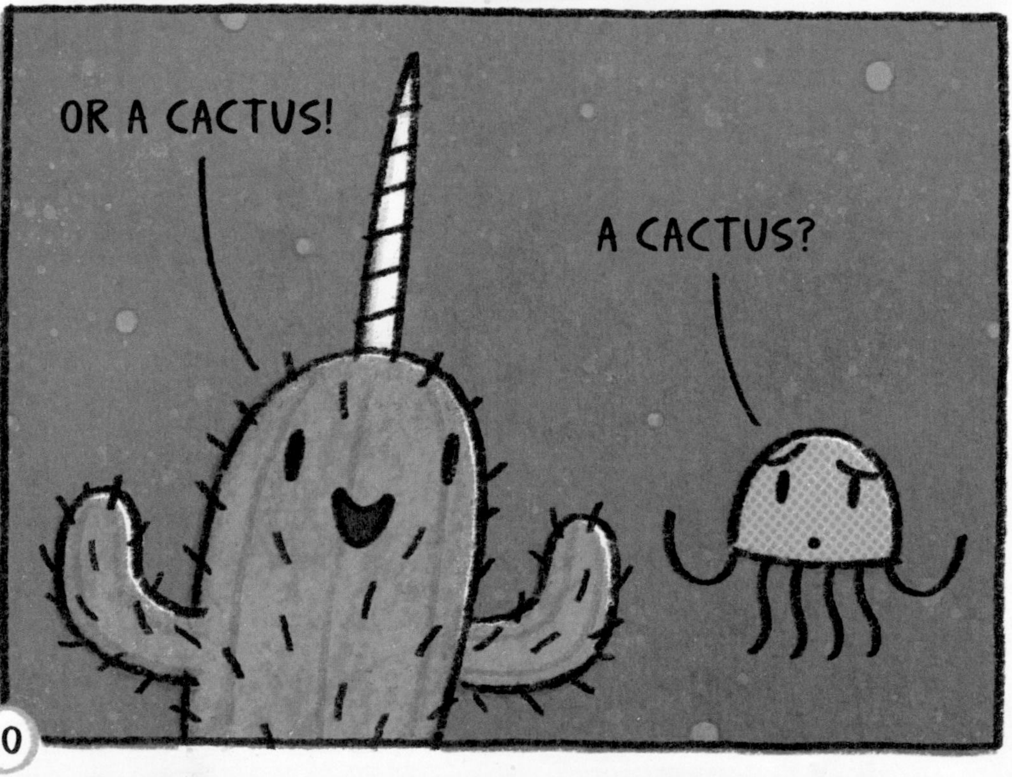
OR A CACTUS!
A CACTUS?

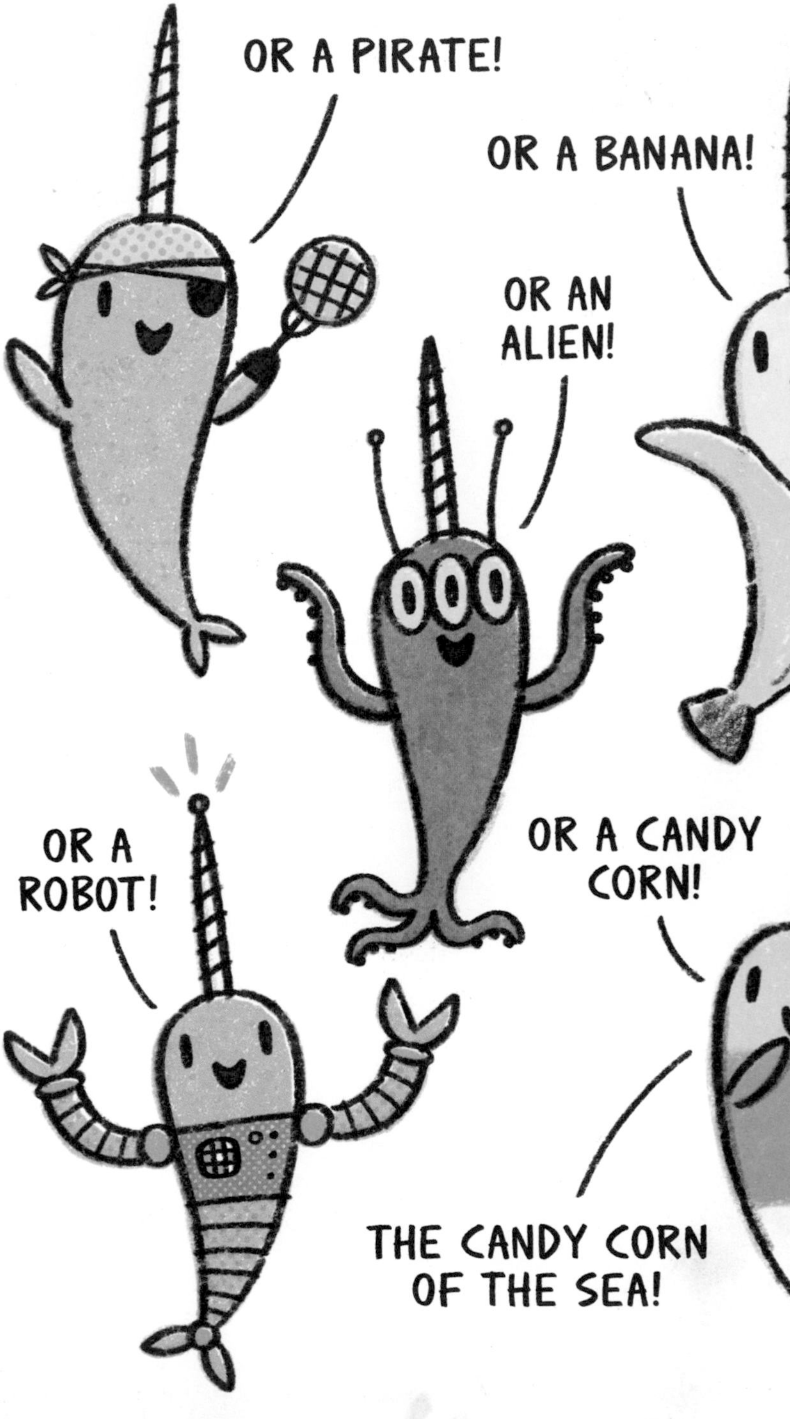

OR A PIRATE!
OR A BANANA!
OR AN ALIEN!
OR A ROBOT!
OR A CANDY CORN!
THE CANDY CORN OF THE SEA!

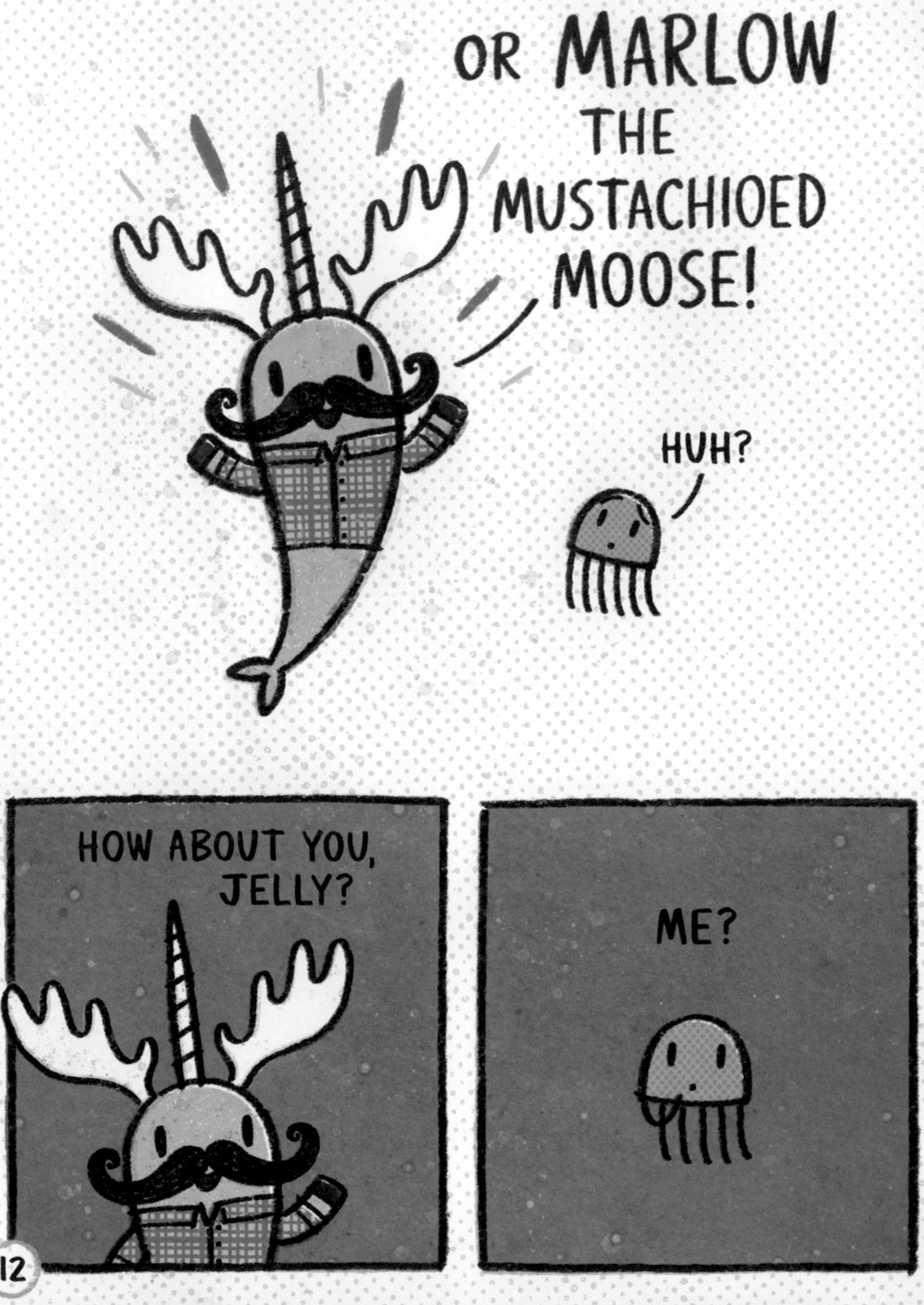
OR MARLOW THE MUSTACHIOED MOOSE!
HUH?
HOW ABOUT YOU, JELLY?
ME?

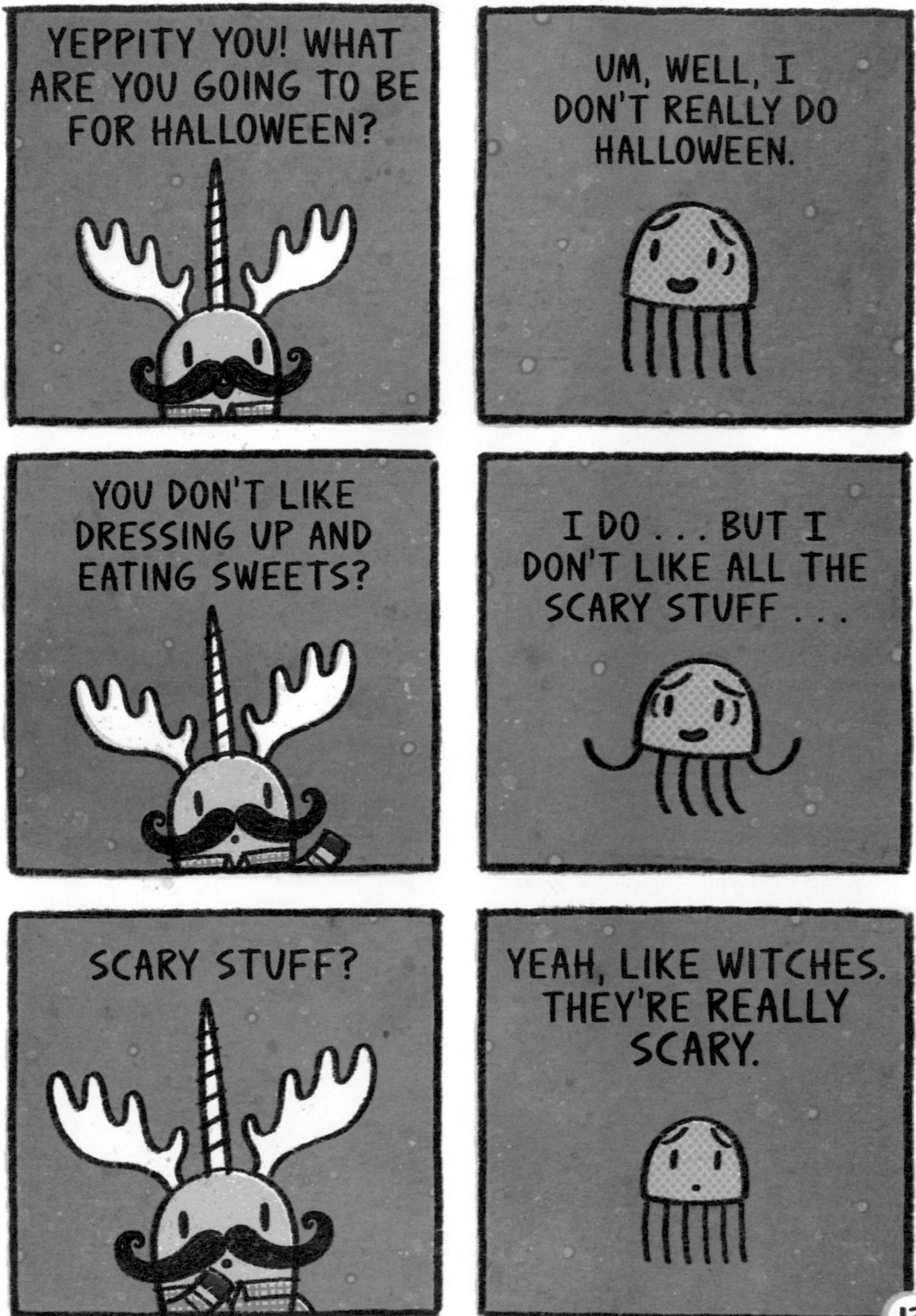
YEPPITY YOU! WHAT ARE YOU GOING TO BE FOR HALLOWEEN?
UM, WELL, I DON'T REALLY DO HALLOWEEN.
YOU DON'T LIKE DRESSING UP AND EATING SWEETS?
I DO . . . BUT I DON'T LIKE ALL THE SCARY STUFF . . .
SCARY STUFF?
YEAH, LIKE WITCHES. THEY'RE REALLY SCARY.

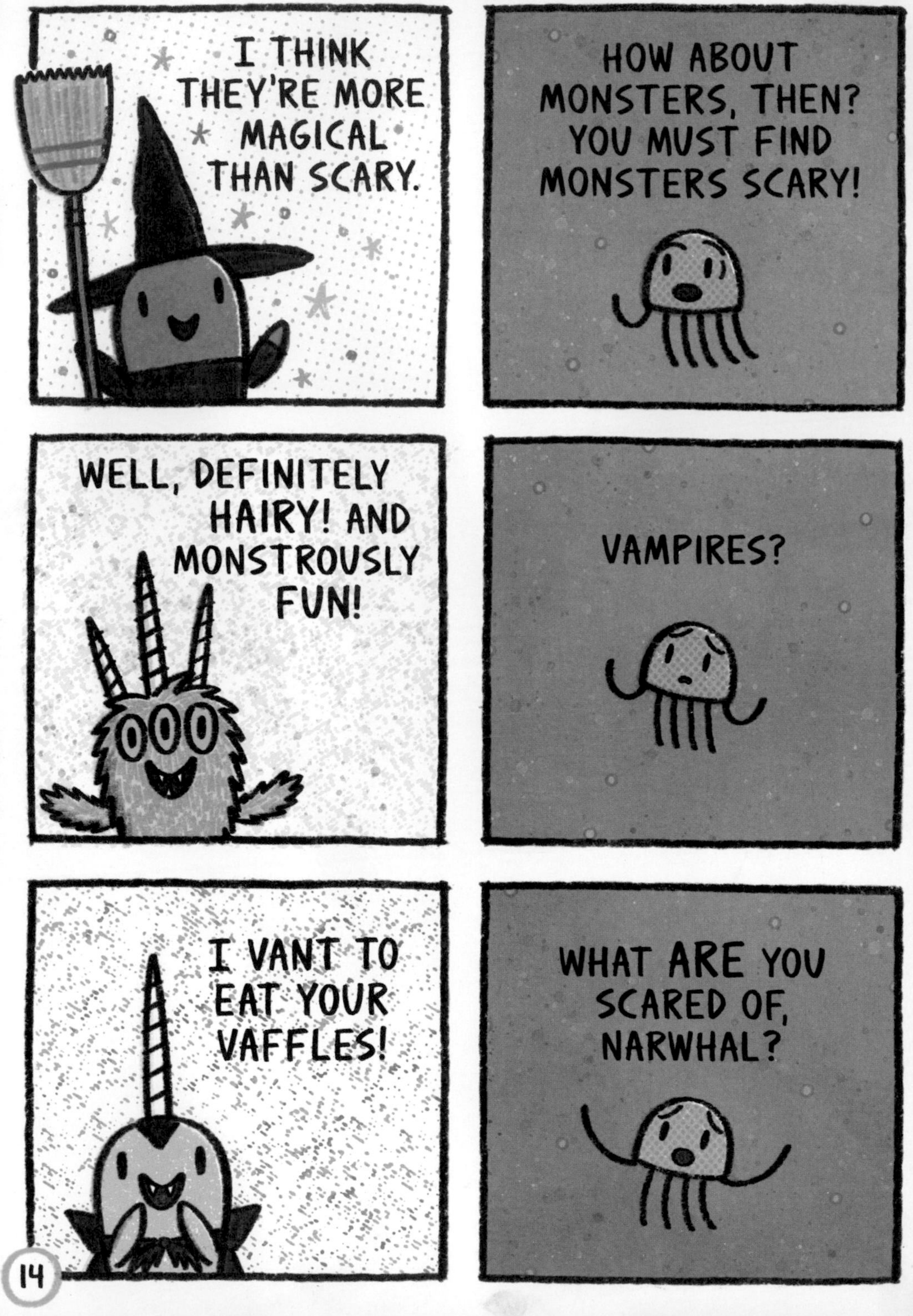
I THINK THEY'RE MORE MAGICAL THAN SCARY.
HOW ABOUT MONSTERS, THEN? YOU MUST FIND MONSTERS SCARY!
WELL, DEFINITELY HAIRY! AND MONSTROUSLY FUN!
VAMPIRES?
I VANT TO EAT YOUR VAFFLES!
WHAT ARE YOU SCARED OF, NARWHAL?

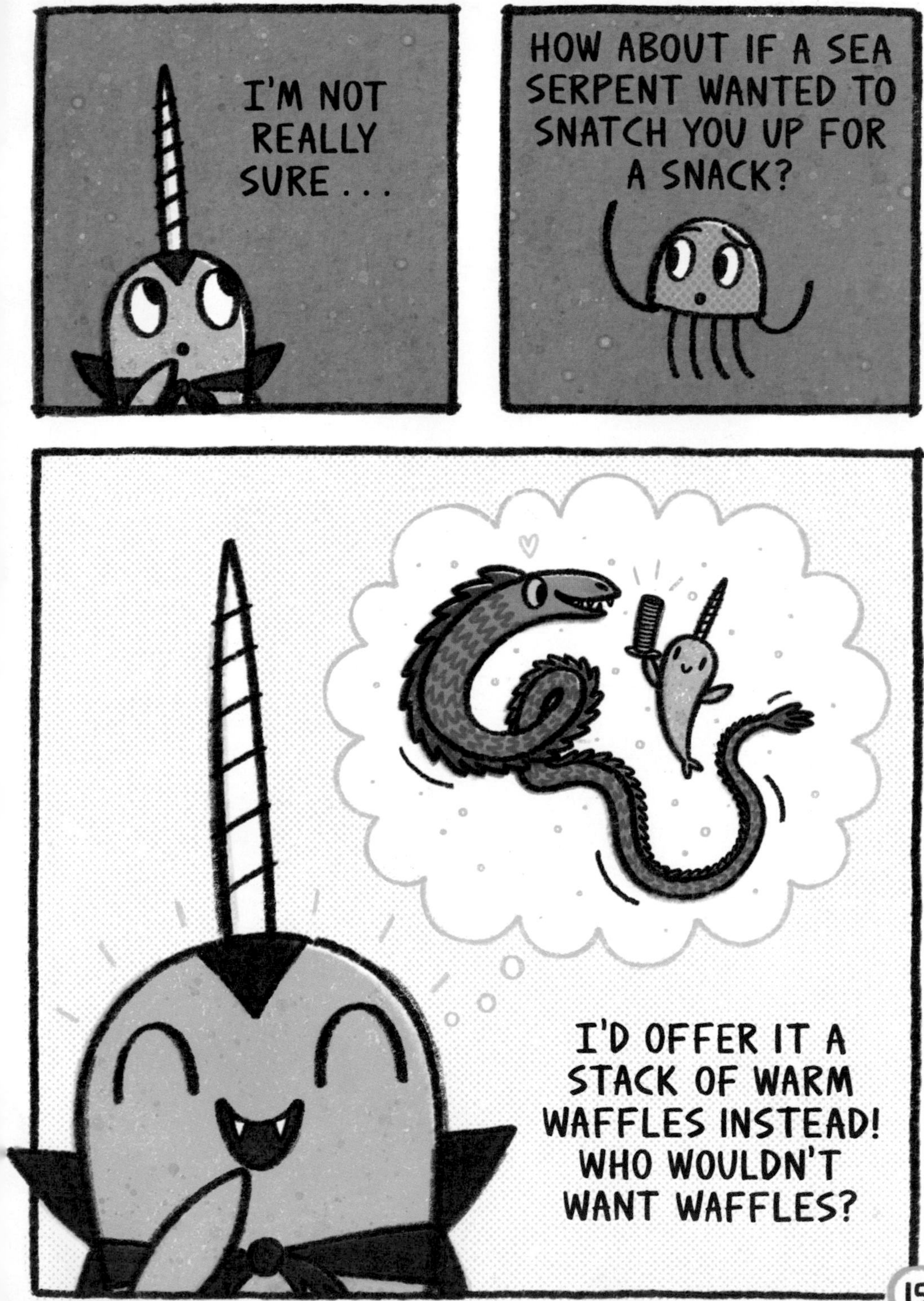
I'M NOT REALLY SURE . . .
HOW ABOUT IF A SEA SERPENT WANTED TO SNATCH YOU UP FOR A SNACK?
I'D OFFER IT A STACK OF WARM WAFFLES INSTEAD! WHO WOULDN'T WANT WAFFLES?

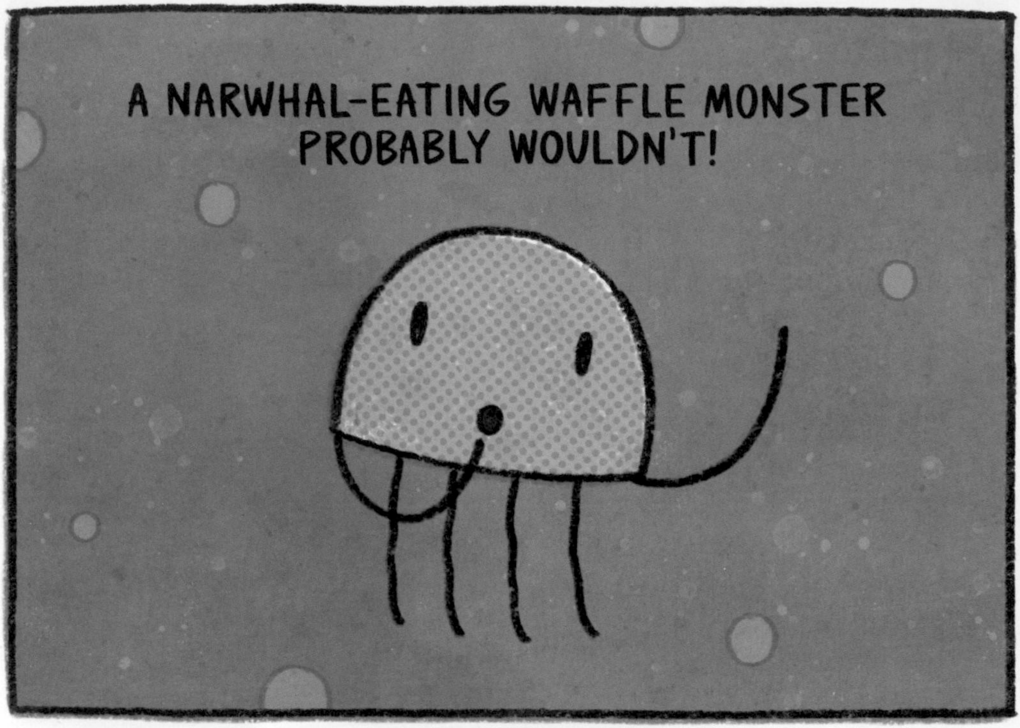
A NARWHAL-EATING WAFFLE MONSTER PROBABLY WOULDN'T!

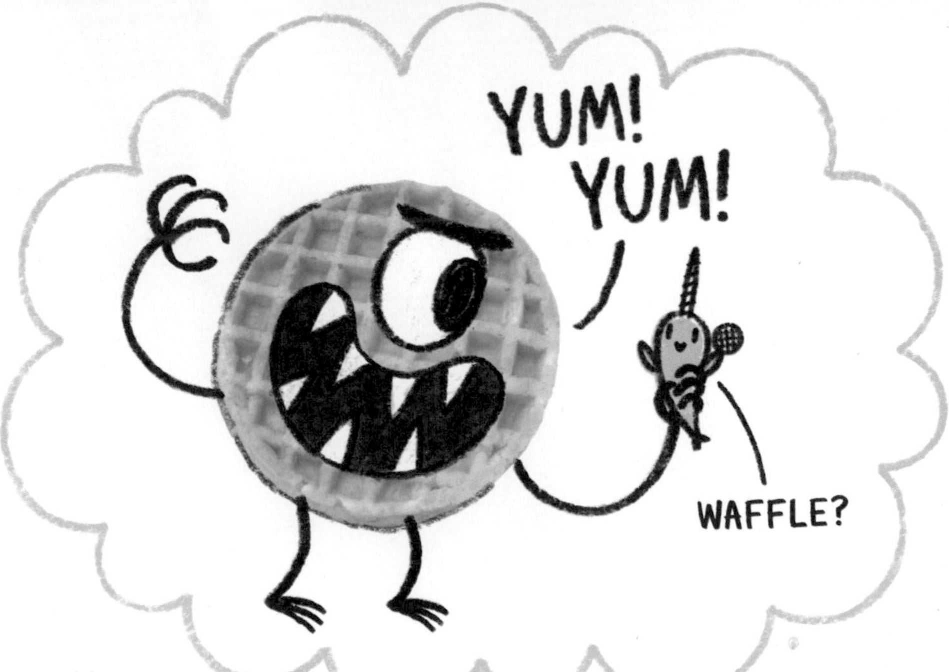
YUM! YUM!
WAFFLE?

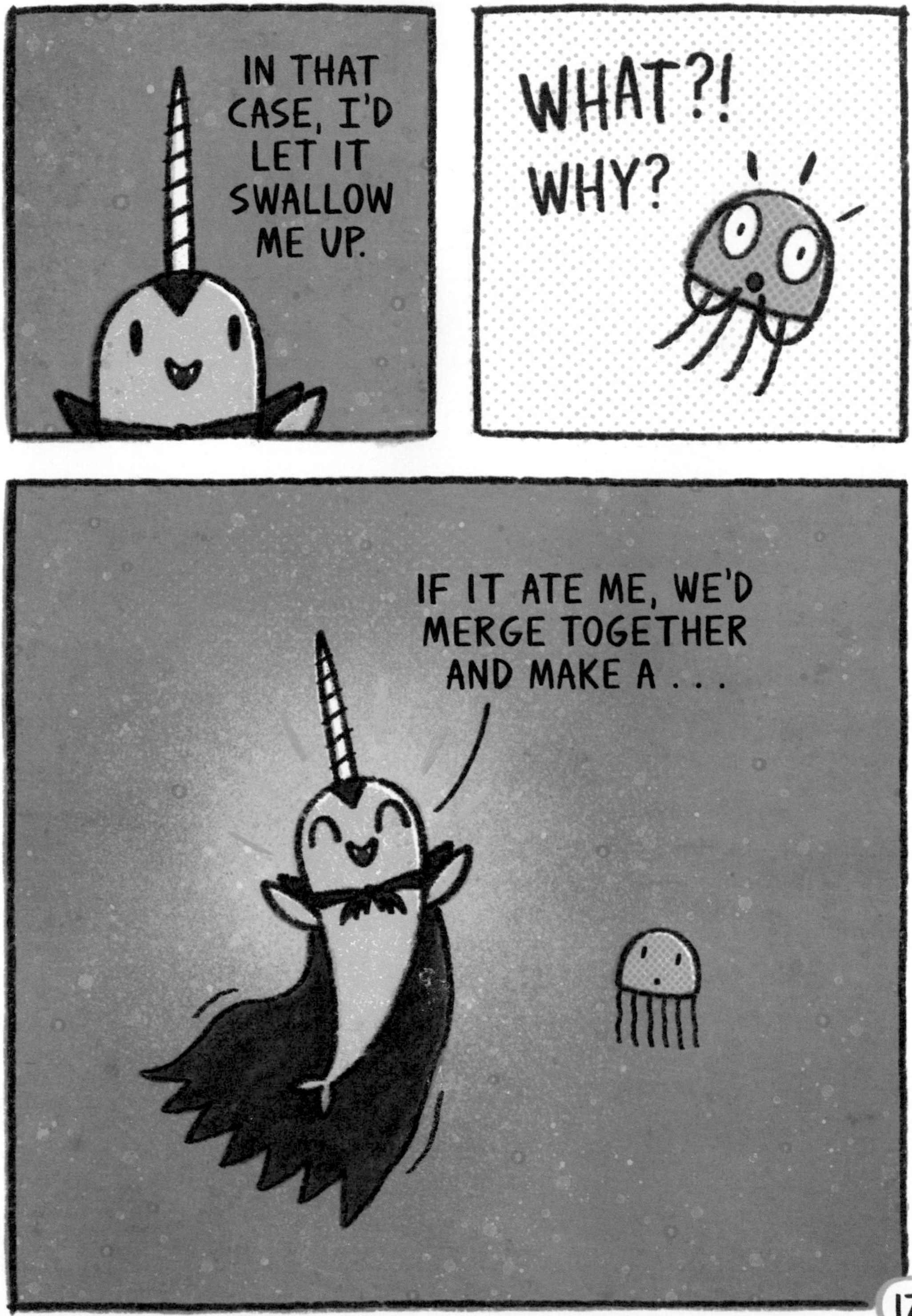
IN THAT CASE, I'D LET IT SWALLOW ME UP.
WHAT?! WHY?
IF IT ATE ME, WE'D MERGE TOGETHER AND MAKE A . . .

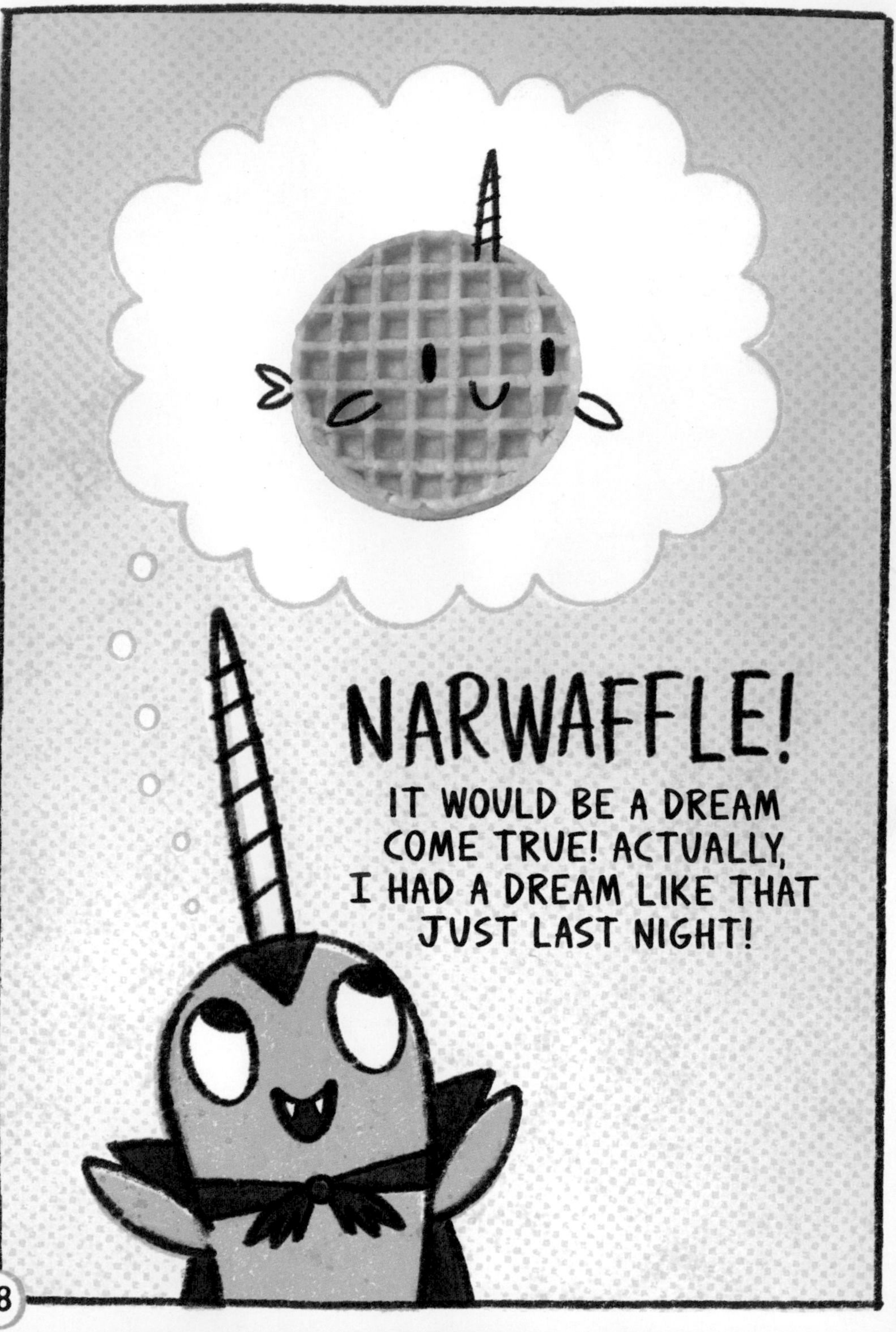
NARWAFFLE!
IT WOULD BE A DREAM COME TRUE! ACTUALLY, I HAD A DREAM LIKE THAT JUST LAST NIGHT!

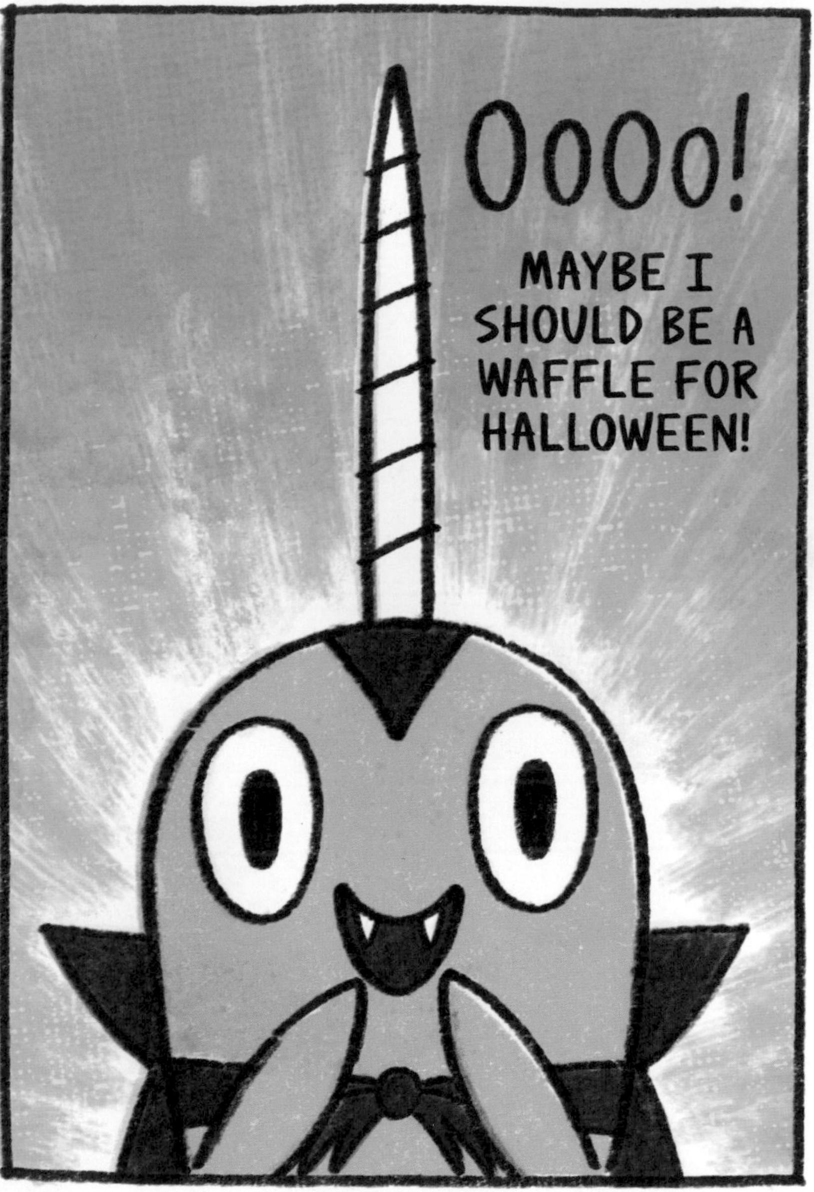
OOOo!
MAYBE I SHOULD BE A WAFFLE FOR HALLOWEEN!

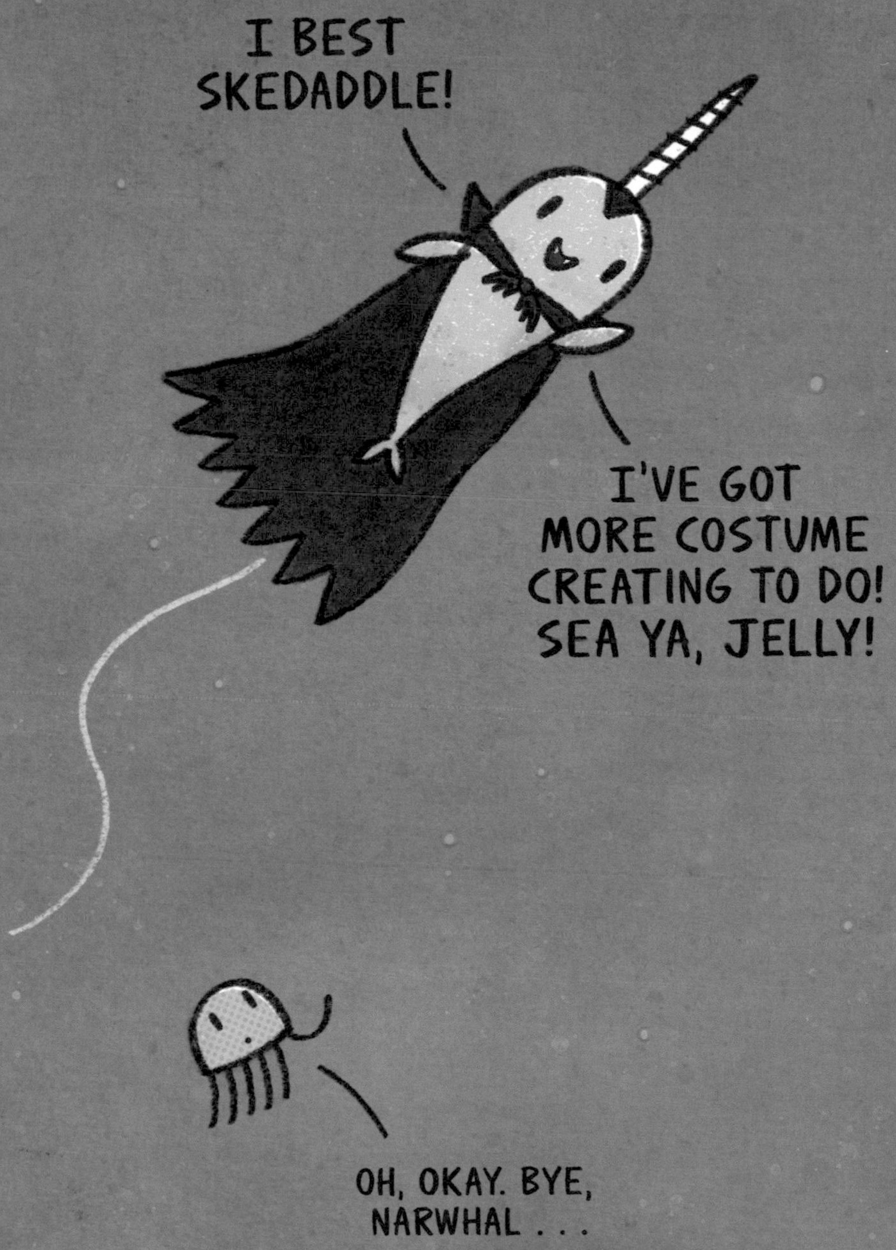
I BEST SKEDADDLE!
I'VE GOT MORE COSTUME CREATING TO DO! SEA YA, JELLY!
OH, OKAY. BYE, NARWHAL . . .

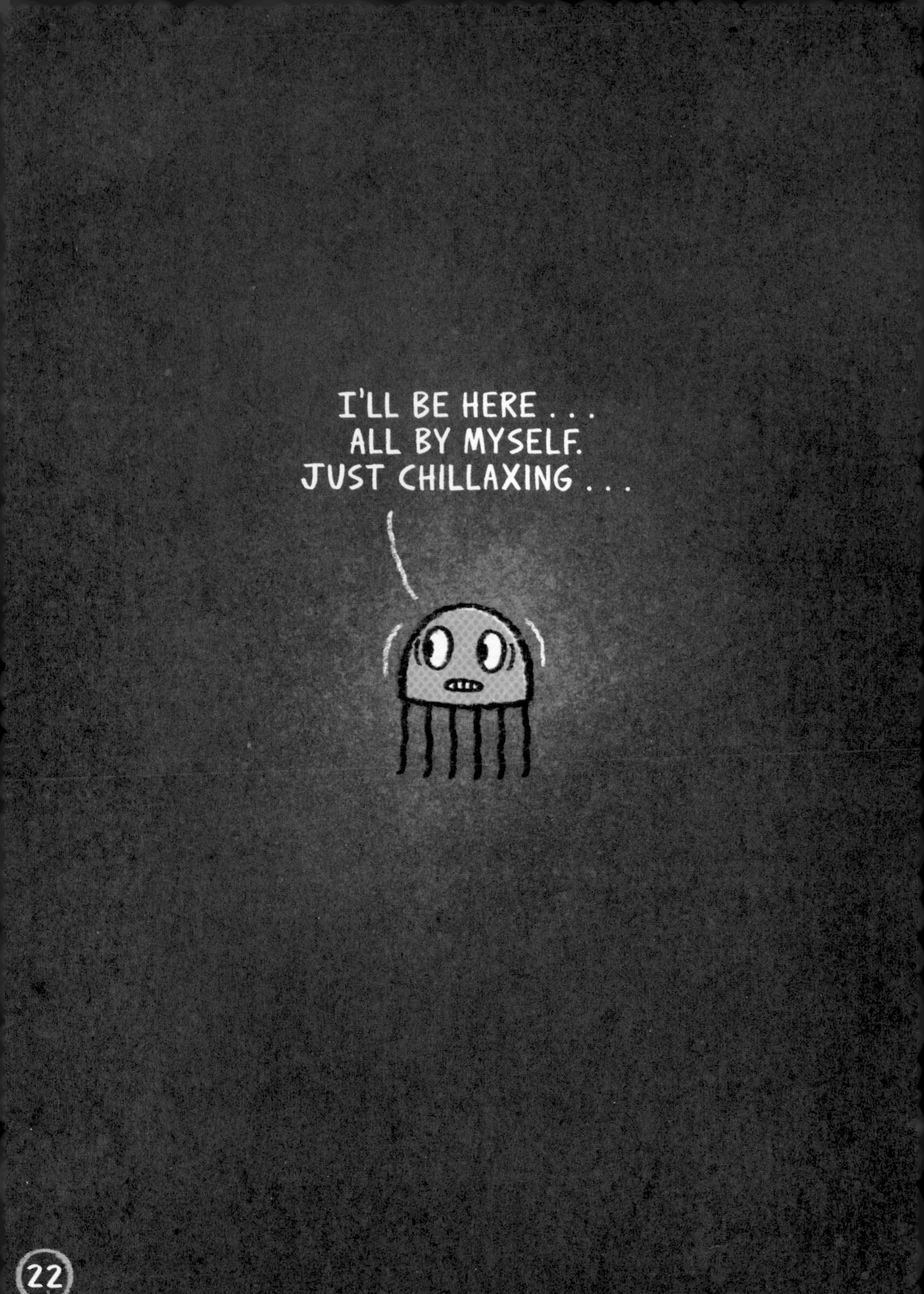
I'LL BE HERE . . .
ALL BY MYSELF.
JUST CHILLAXING . . .

FANG TASTIC
FACTS

DO YOU FIND ANY OF THESE
REAL-LIFE SEA CREATURES SCARY?

THE GOBLIN SHARK
IS A RARE SPECIES OF
DEEP-SEA SHARK.

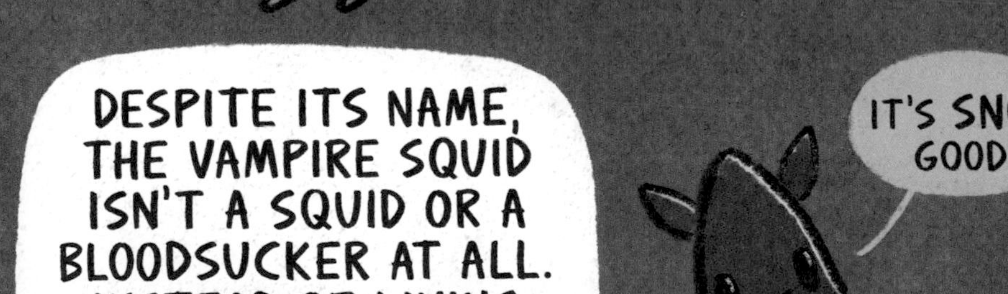

DON'T WORRY!
I WON'T BE GOBLIN
YOU UP. I PREFER
CRABS . . .

DESPITE ITS NAME,
THE VAMPIRE SQUID
ISN'T A SQUID OR A
BLOODSUCKER AT ALL.
INSTEAD OF LIVING
THINGS, IT EATS
MARINE SNOW, A KIND
OF ORGANIC MATTER.

IT'S SNOW
GOOD!

EVEN THOUGH THE GIANT PHANTOM JELLYFISH CAN REACH UP TO 33 FEET LONG (10 METERS), IT IS SELDOM SEEN.

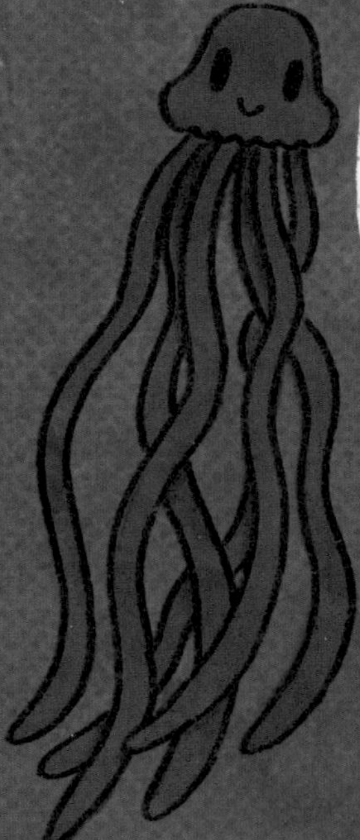

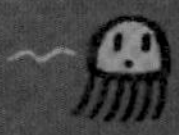
I HAVE A STRANGE FEELING THAT SOMETHING IS FOLLOWING ME . . .

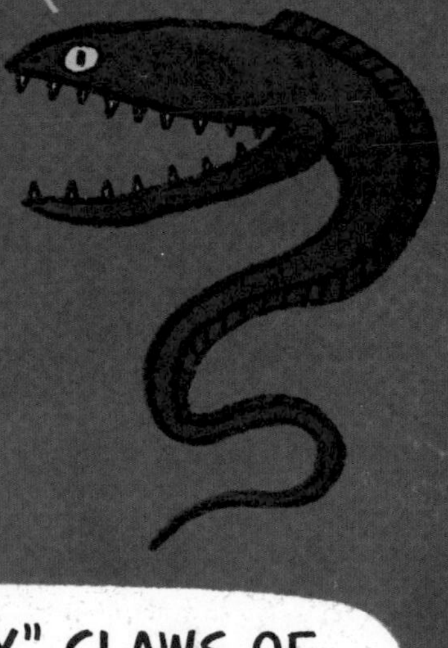
I'M GREAT AT EATING CONTESTS!

THE GULPER EEL'S MOUTH IS ABLE TO OPEN WIDE ENOUGH TO EAT THINGS MUCH LARGER THAN ITSELF.

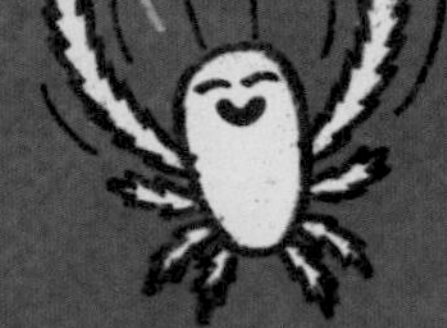
COME HAIR, FOOD!

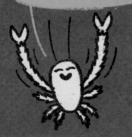

THE "HAIRY" CLAWS OF THE YETI CRAB ARE USED TO CATCH ITS MAIN FOOD SOURCE: BACTERIA.

THE GREAT GURGLE

SIX SECONDS LATER . . .

MAYBE I SHOULD FIND A LITTLE
HIDEY-HOLE AND HUNKER DOWN
UNTIL HALLOWEEN IS OVER.

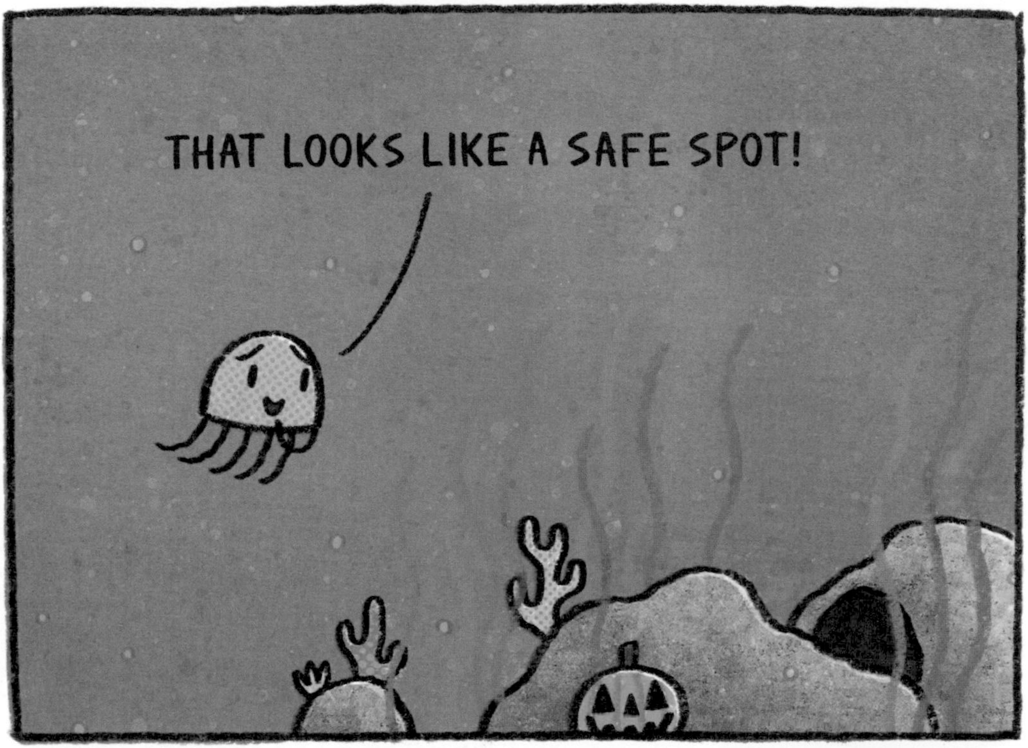
THAT LOOKS LIKE A SAFE SPOT!

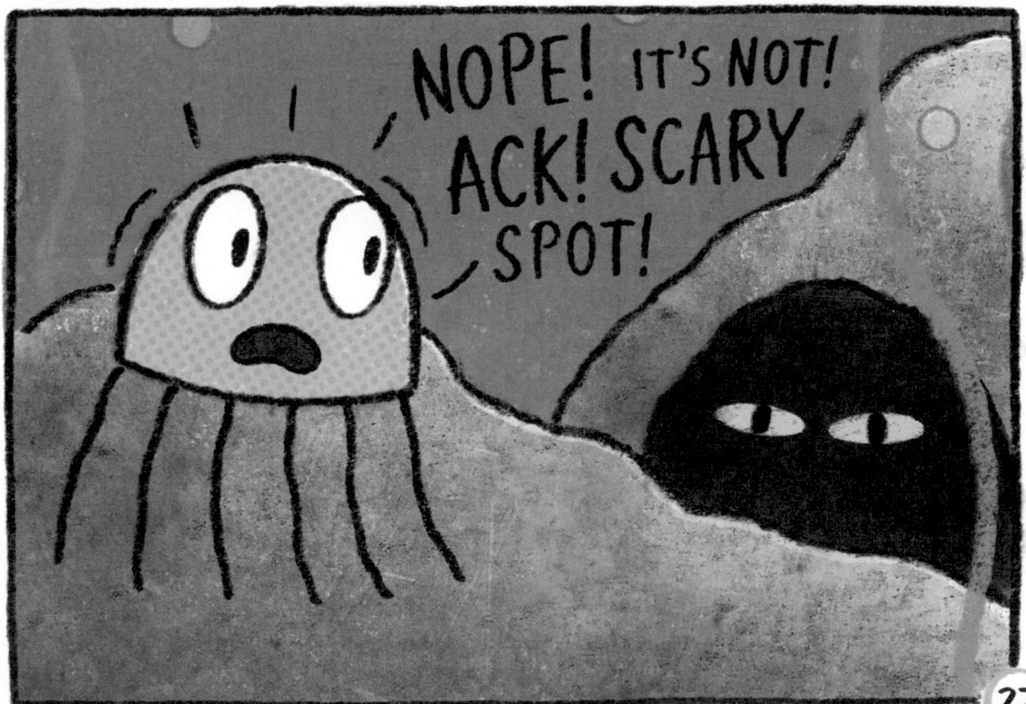
NOPE! IT'S NOT!
ACK! SCARY SPOT!

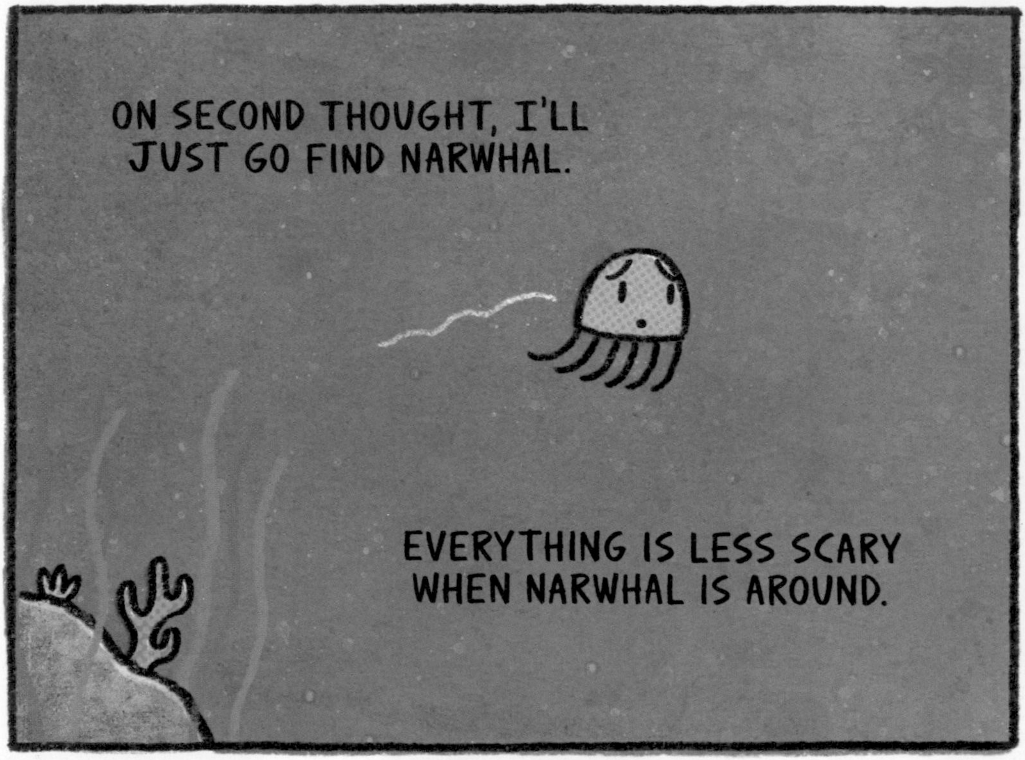
ON SECOND THOUGHT, I'LL JUST GO FIND NARWHAL.
EVERYTHING IS LESS SCARY WHEN NARWHAL IS AROUND.

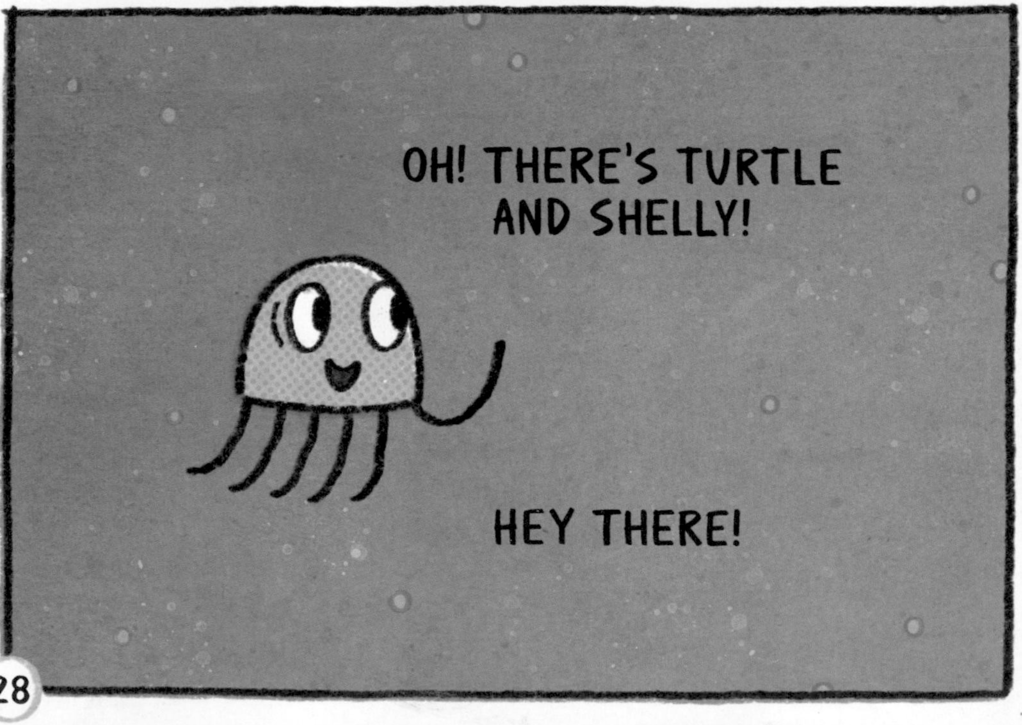
OH! THERE'S TURTLE AND SHELLY!
HEY THERE!

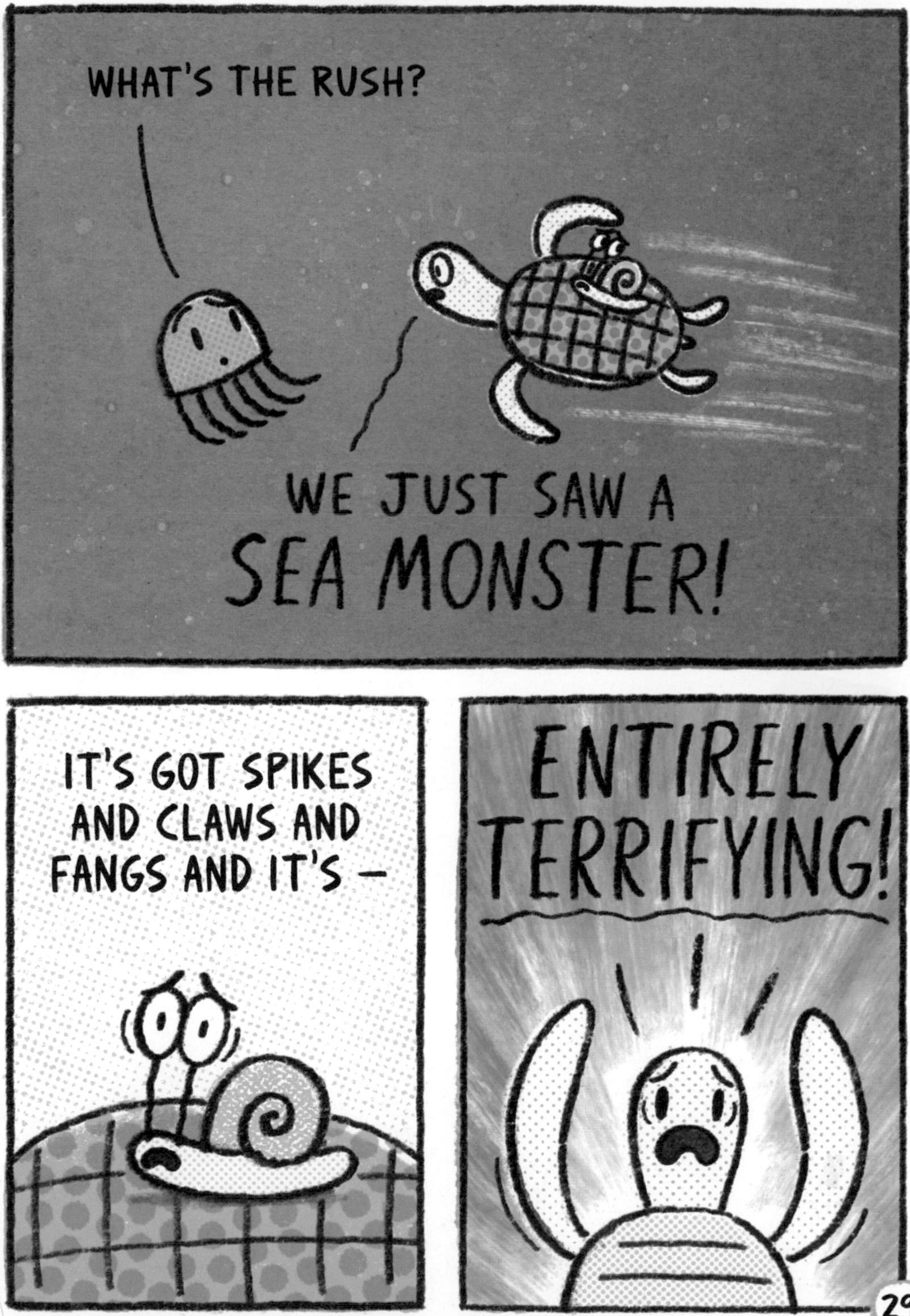
WHAT'S THE RUSH?
WE JUST SAW A SEA MONSTER!
IT'S GOT SPIKES AND CLAWS AND FANGS AND IT'S —
ENTIRELY TERRIFYING!

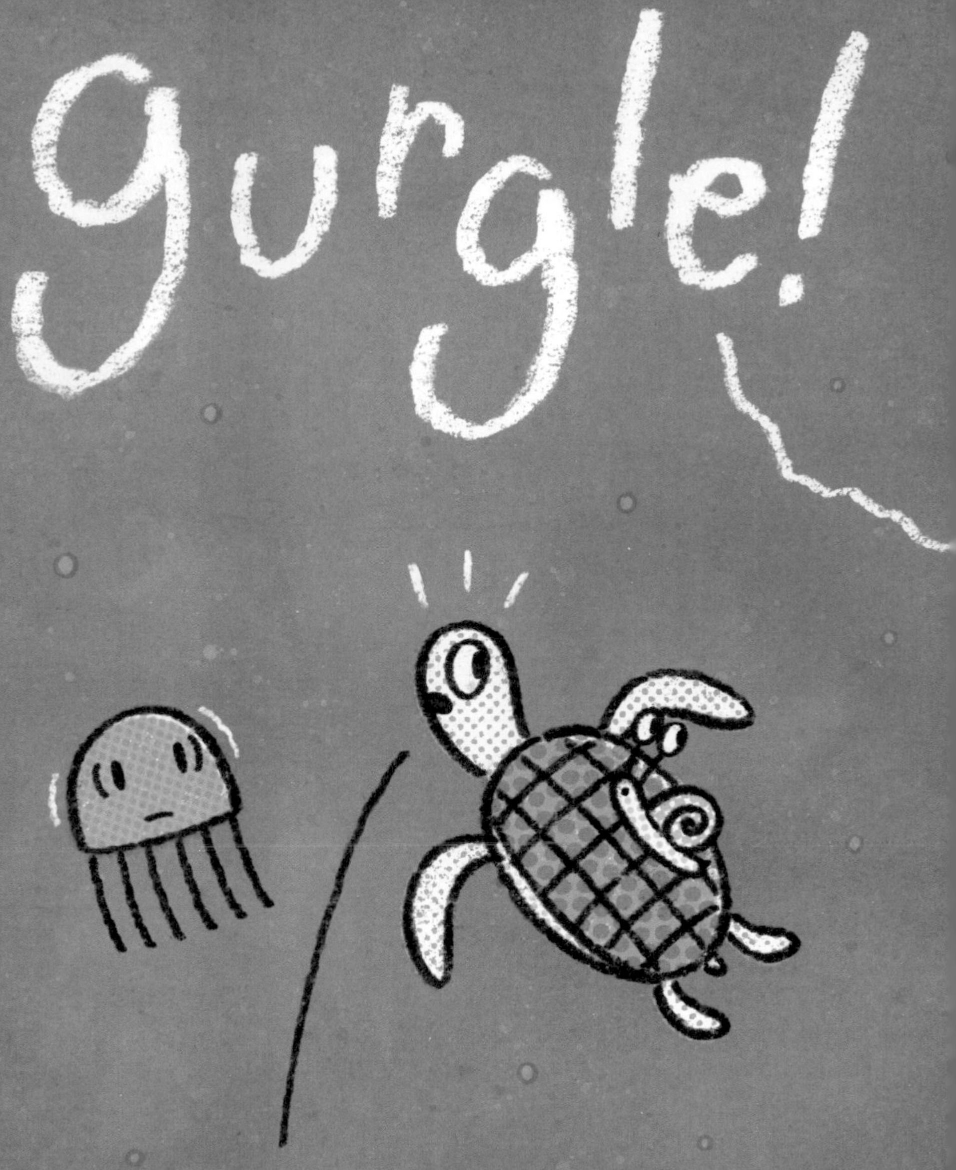
gurgle!

IT ALSO SOUNDS SUPER HUNGRY.
LET'S KEEP SWIMMING, SHELLY!

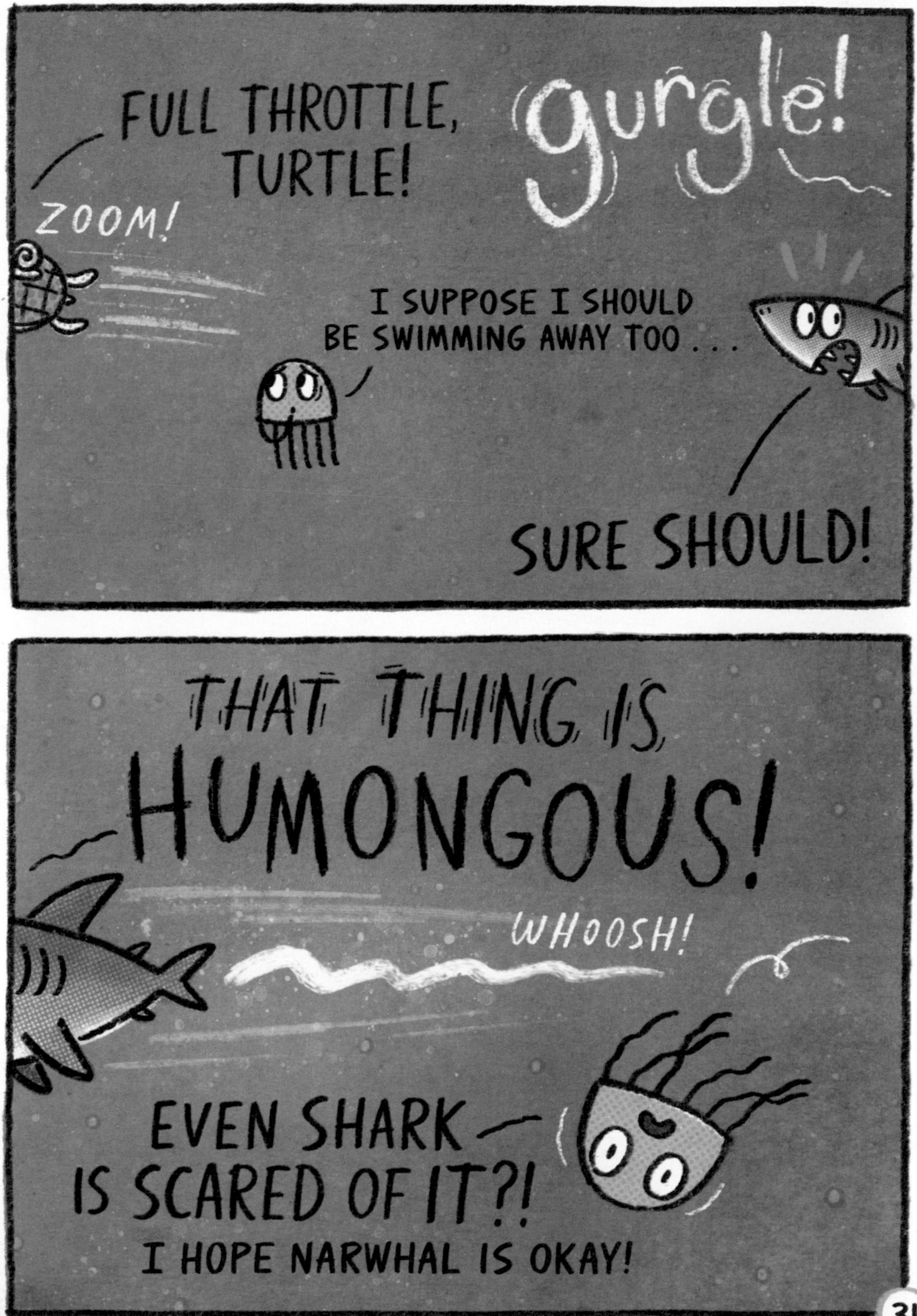

FULL THROTTLE, TURTLE!
ZOOM!
gurgle!
I SUPPOSE I SHOULD BE SWIMMING AWAY TOO . . .
SURE SHOULD!
THAT THING IS HUMONGOUS!
WHOOSH!
EVEN SHARK IS SCARED OF IT?!
I HOPE NARWHAL IS OKAY!

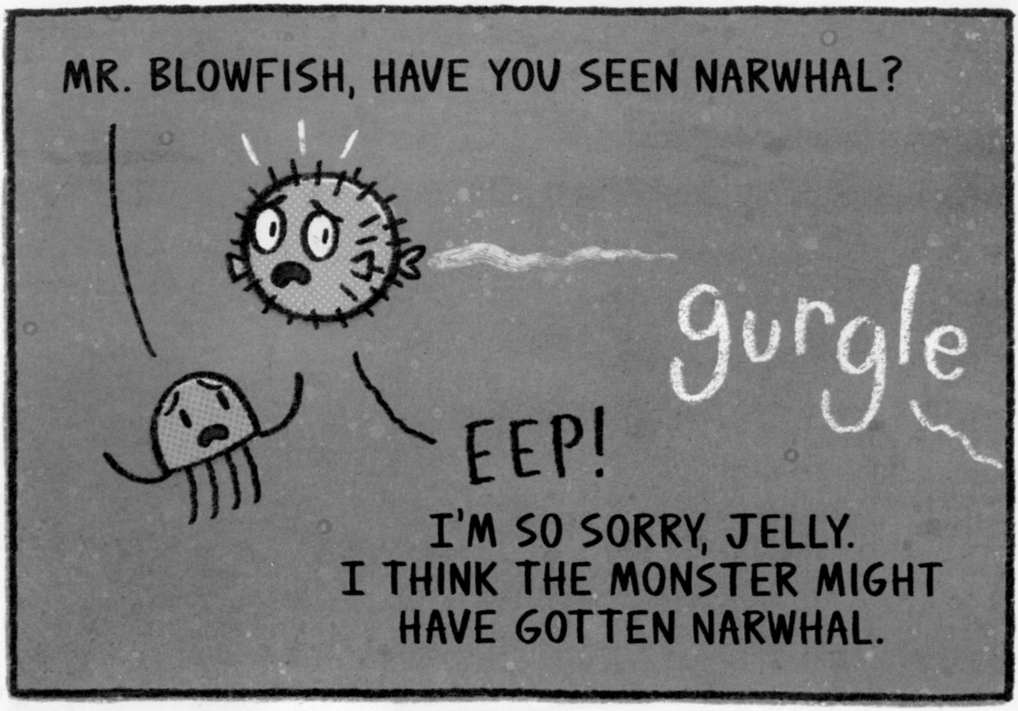
MR. BLOWFISH, HAVE YOU SEEN NARWHAL?
gurgle
EEP!
I'M SO SORRY, JELLY.
I THINK THE MONSTER MIGHT
HAVE GOTTEN NARWHAL.

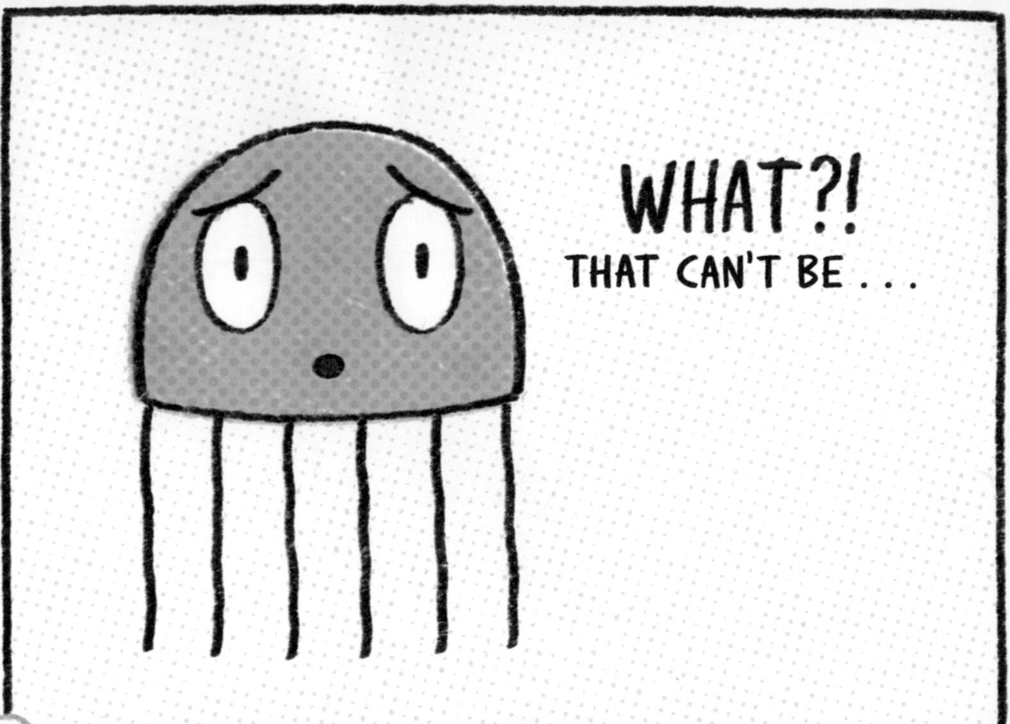
WHAT?!
THAT CAN'T BE . . .

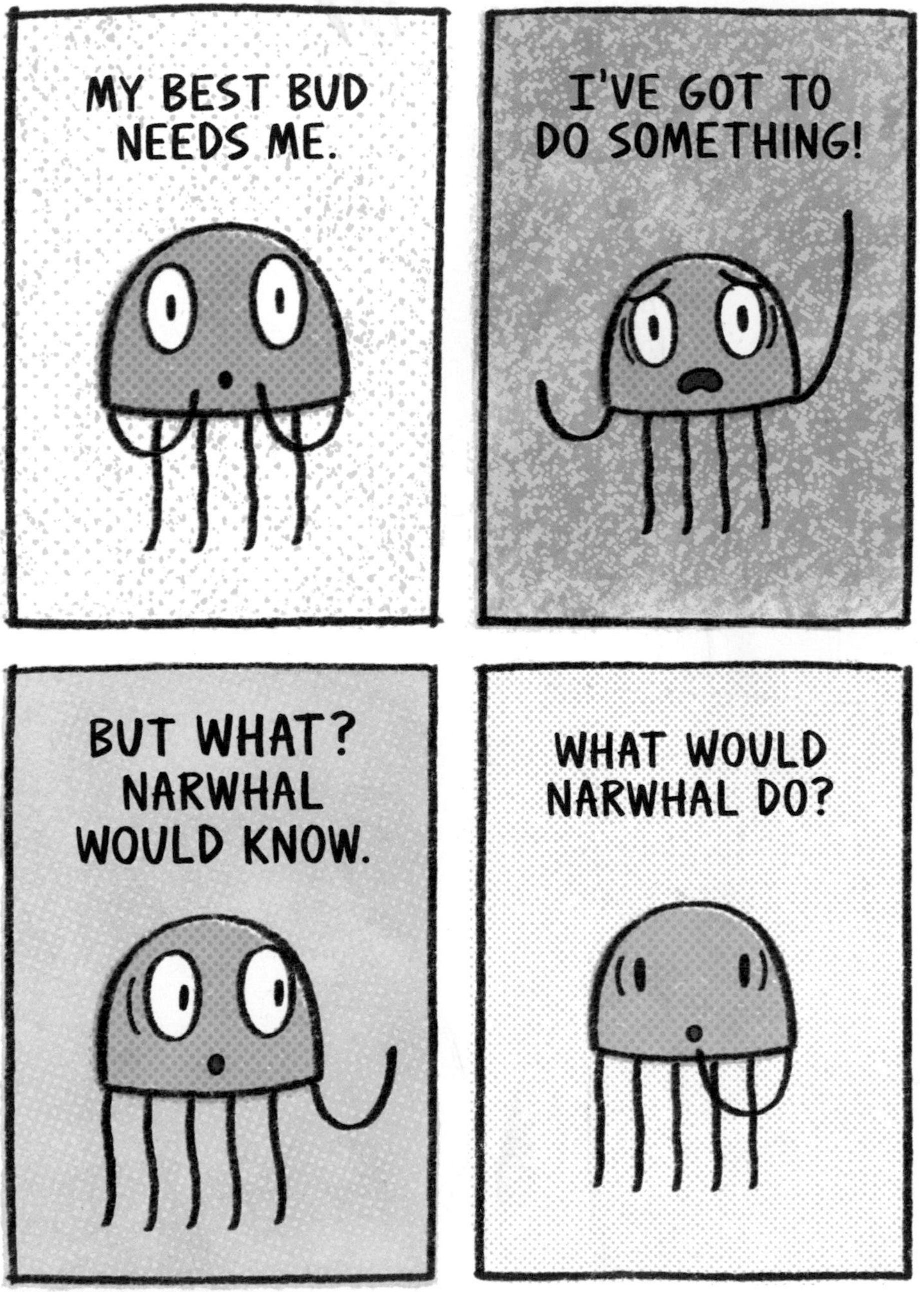
MY BEST BUD NEEDS ME.
I'VE GOT TO DO SOMETHING!
BUT WHAT? NARWHAL WOULD KNOW.
WHAT WOULD NARWHAL DO?

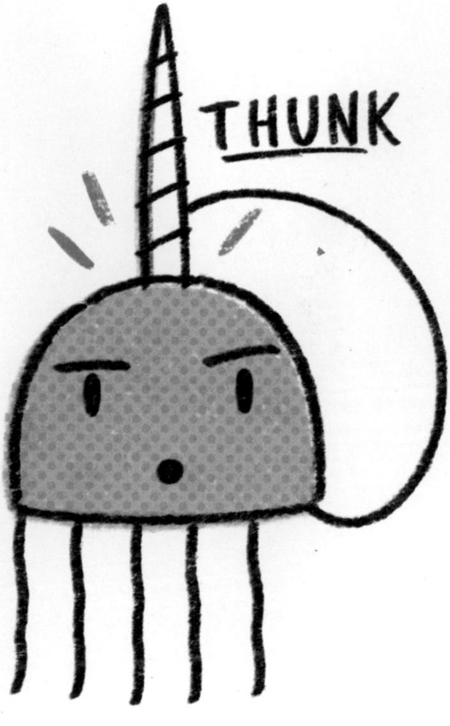
THUNK

I'VE GOT TO THINK LIKE NARWHAL.

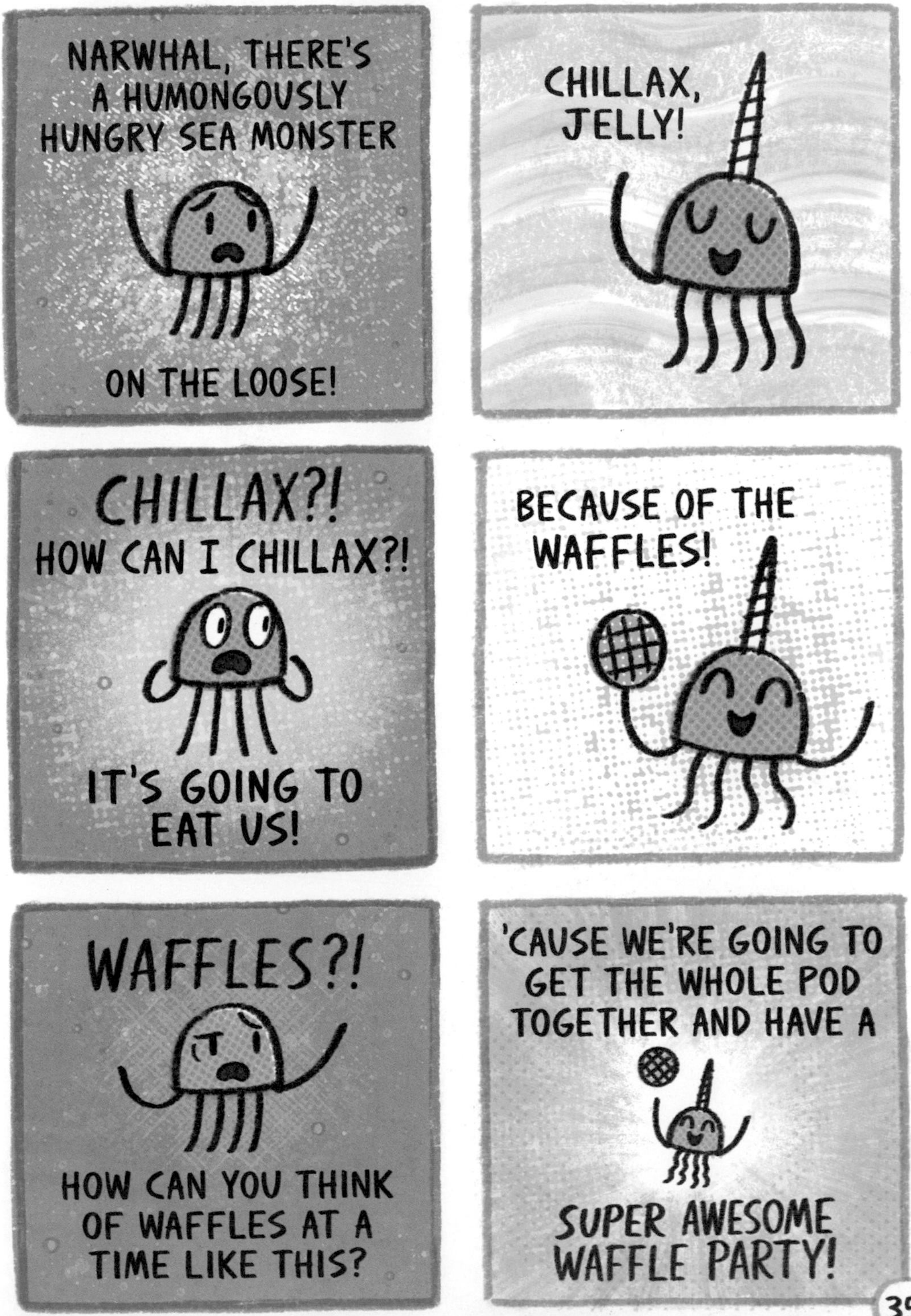
NARWHAL, THERE'S A HUMONGOUSLY HUNGRY SEA MONSTER
ON THE LOOSE!
CHILLAX, JELLY!
CHILLAX?!
HOW CAN I CHILLAX?!
IT'S GOING TO EAT US!
BECAUSE OF THE WAFFLES!
WAFFLES?!
HOW CAN YOU THINK OF WAFFLES AT A TIME LIKE THIS?
'CAUSE WE'RE GOING TO GET THE WHOLE POD TOGETHER AND HAVE A
SUPER AWESOME WAFFLE PARTY!

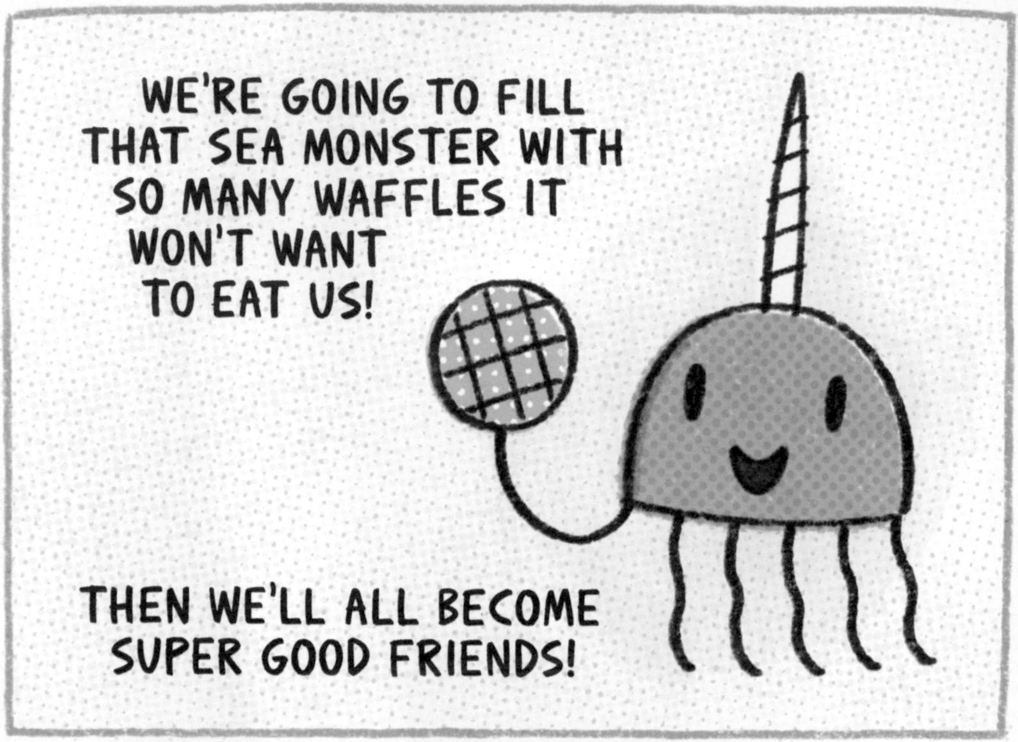
WE'RE GOING TO FILL THAT SEA MONSTER WITH SO MANY WAFFLES IT WON'T WANT TO EAT US!
THEN WE'LL ALL BECOME SUPER GOOD FRIENDS!

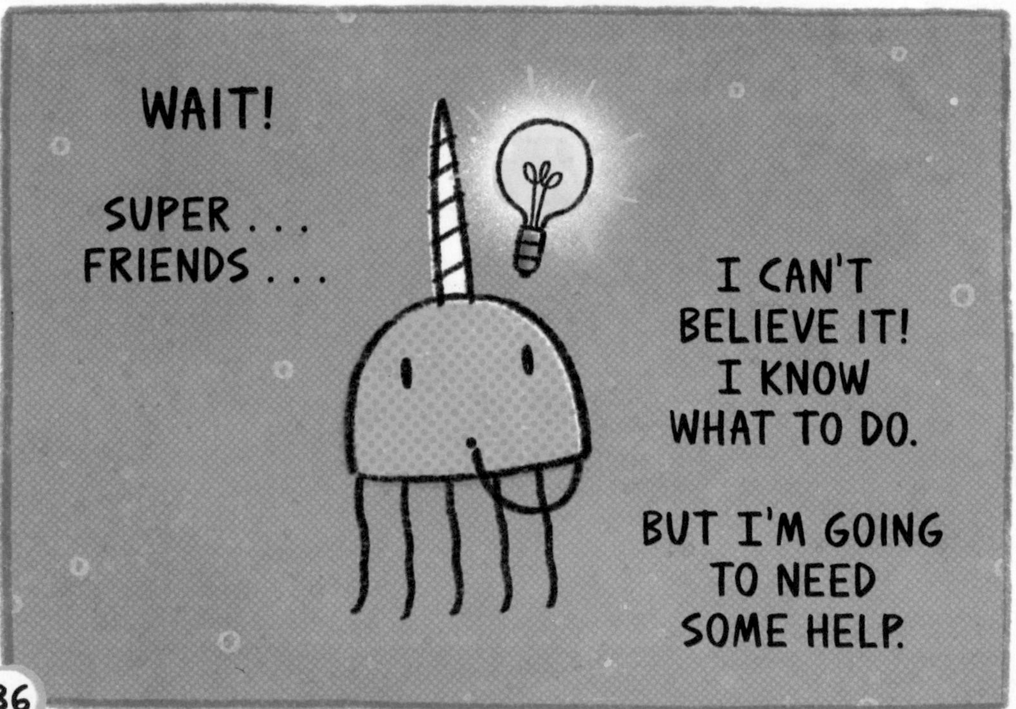
WAIT!
SUPER . . . FRIENDS . . .
I CAN'T BELIEVE IT! I KNOW WHAT TO DO.
BUT I'M GOING TO NEED SOME HELP.

SOME OF THE SUPER SORT.

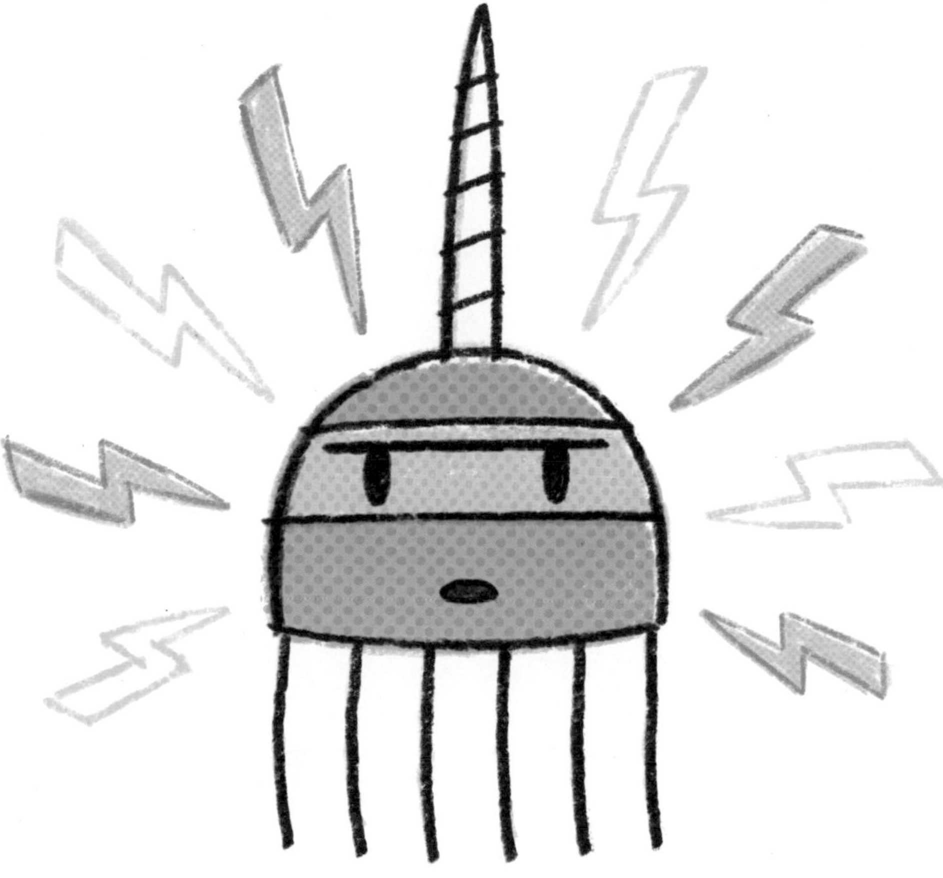

JELLY JOLT

IS BACK.

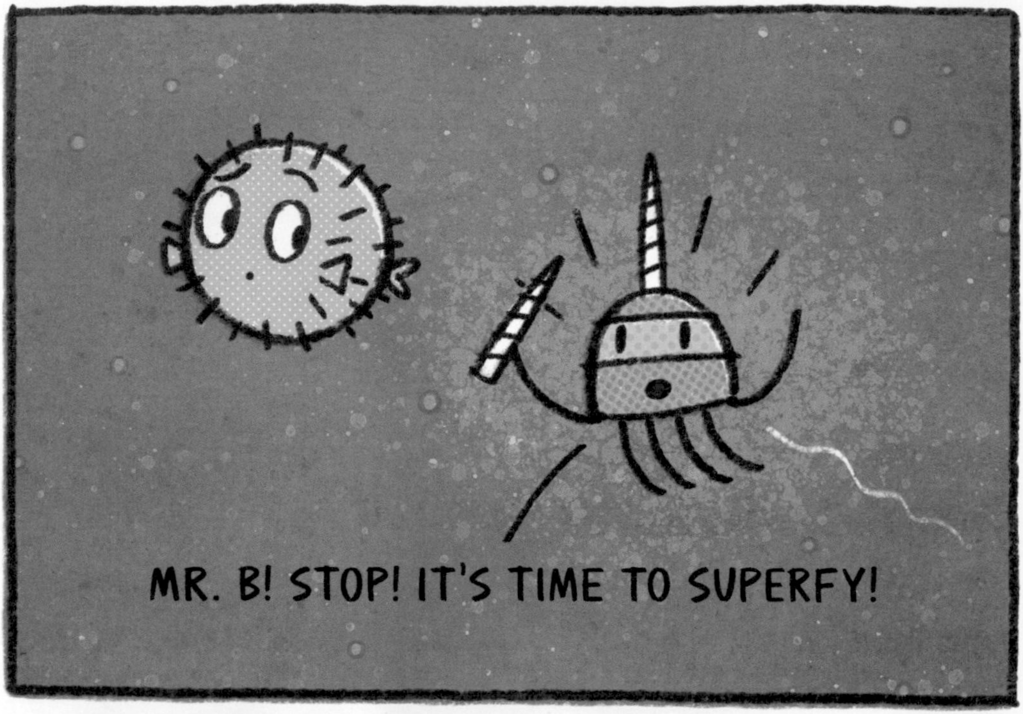
MR. B! STOP! IT'S TIME TO SUPERFY!

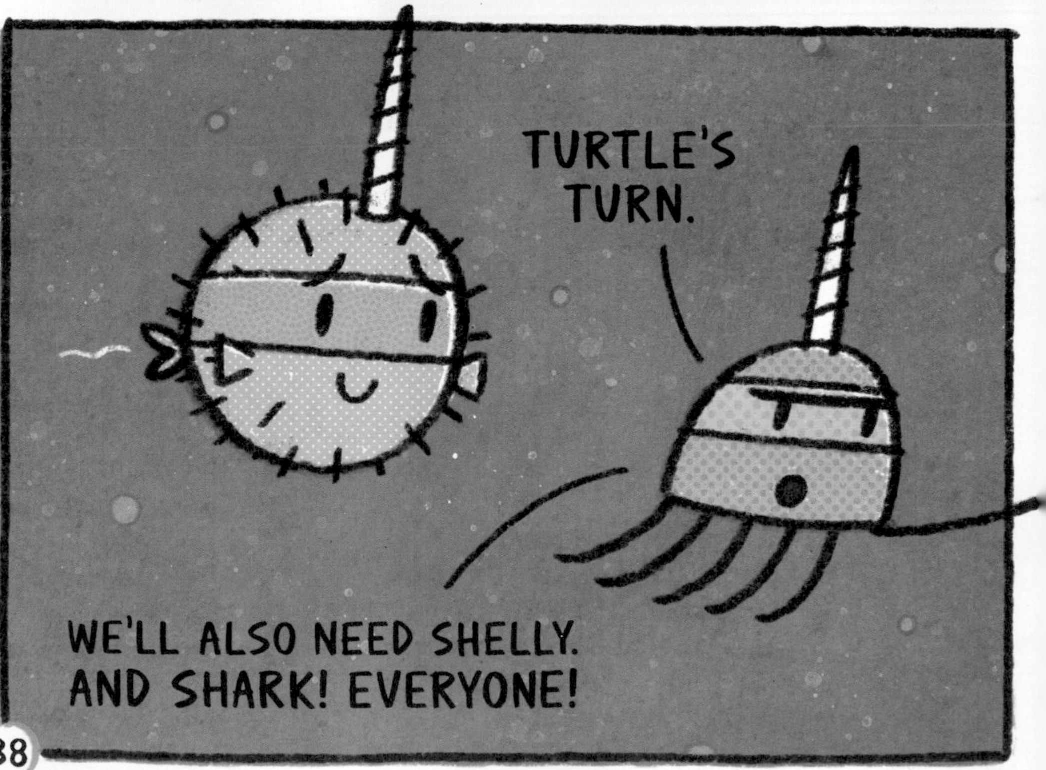
TURTLE'S TURN.
WE'LL ALSO NEED SHELLY. AND SHARK! EVERYONE!

MONTAGE TIME!

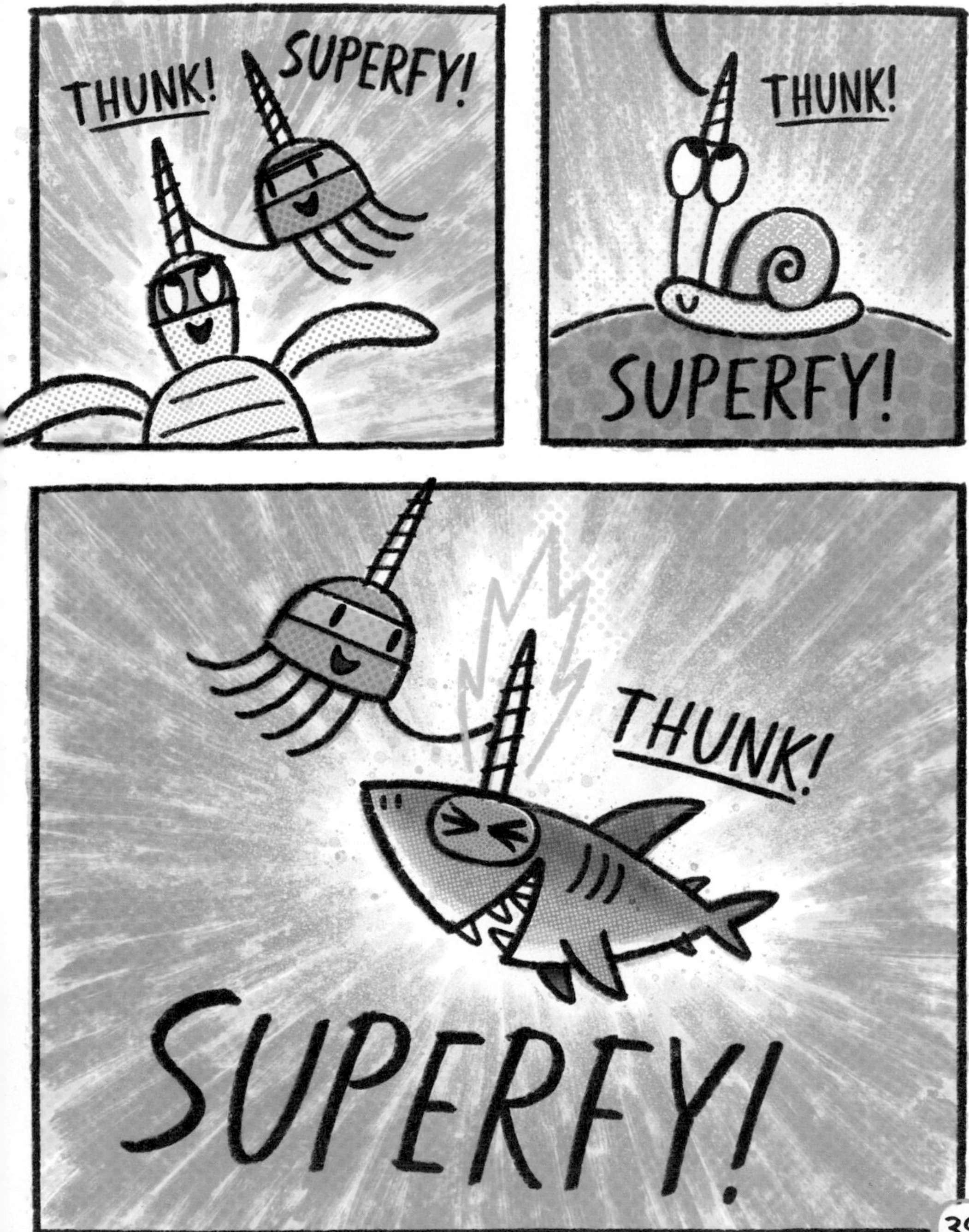

THUNK!
SUPERFY!
THUNK!
SUPERFY!
THUNK!
SUPERFY!

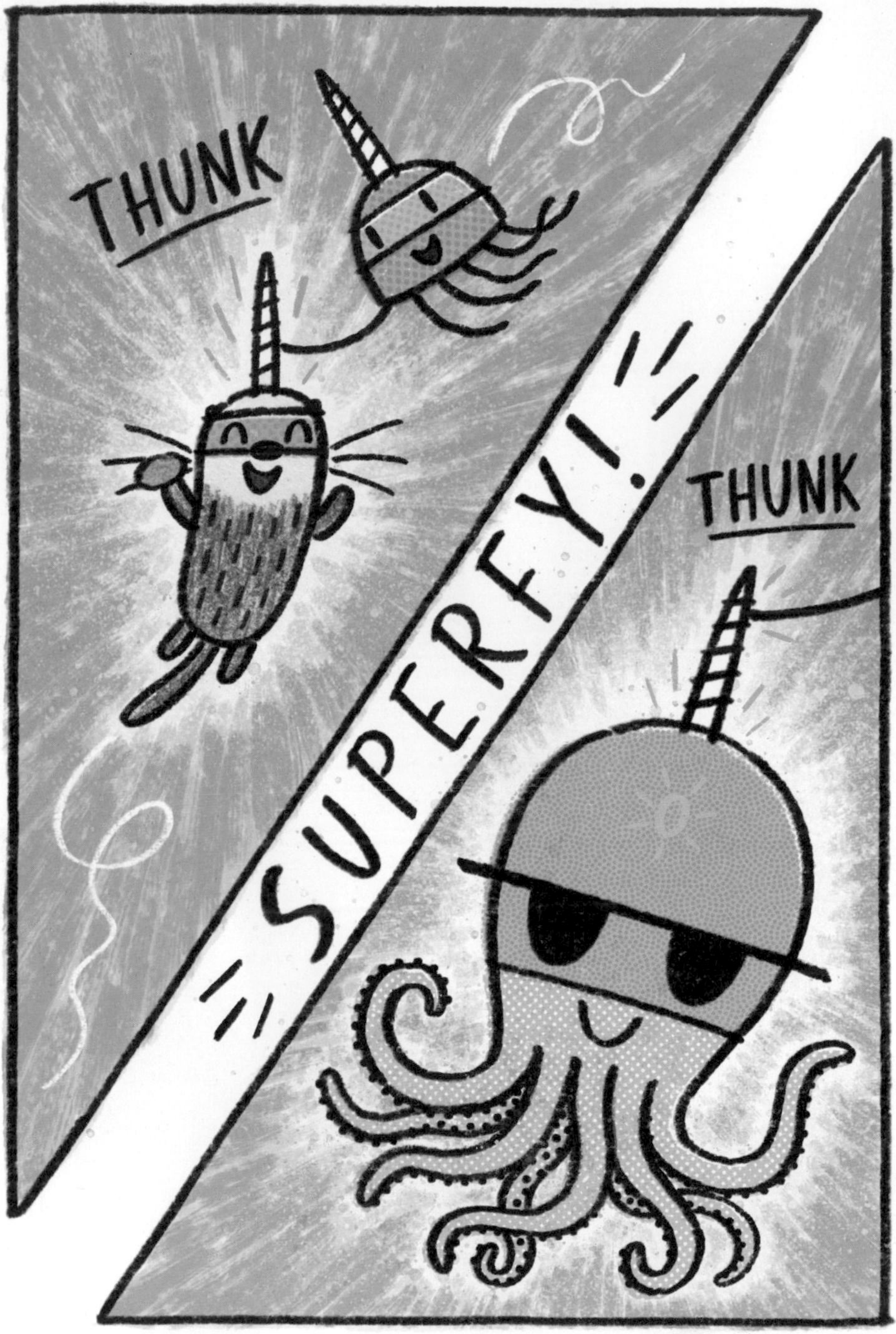
THUNK
SUPERFY!
THUNK

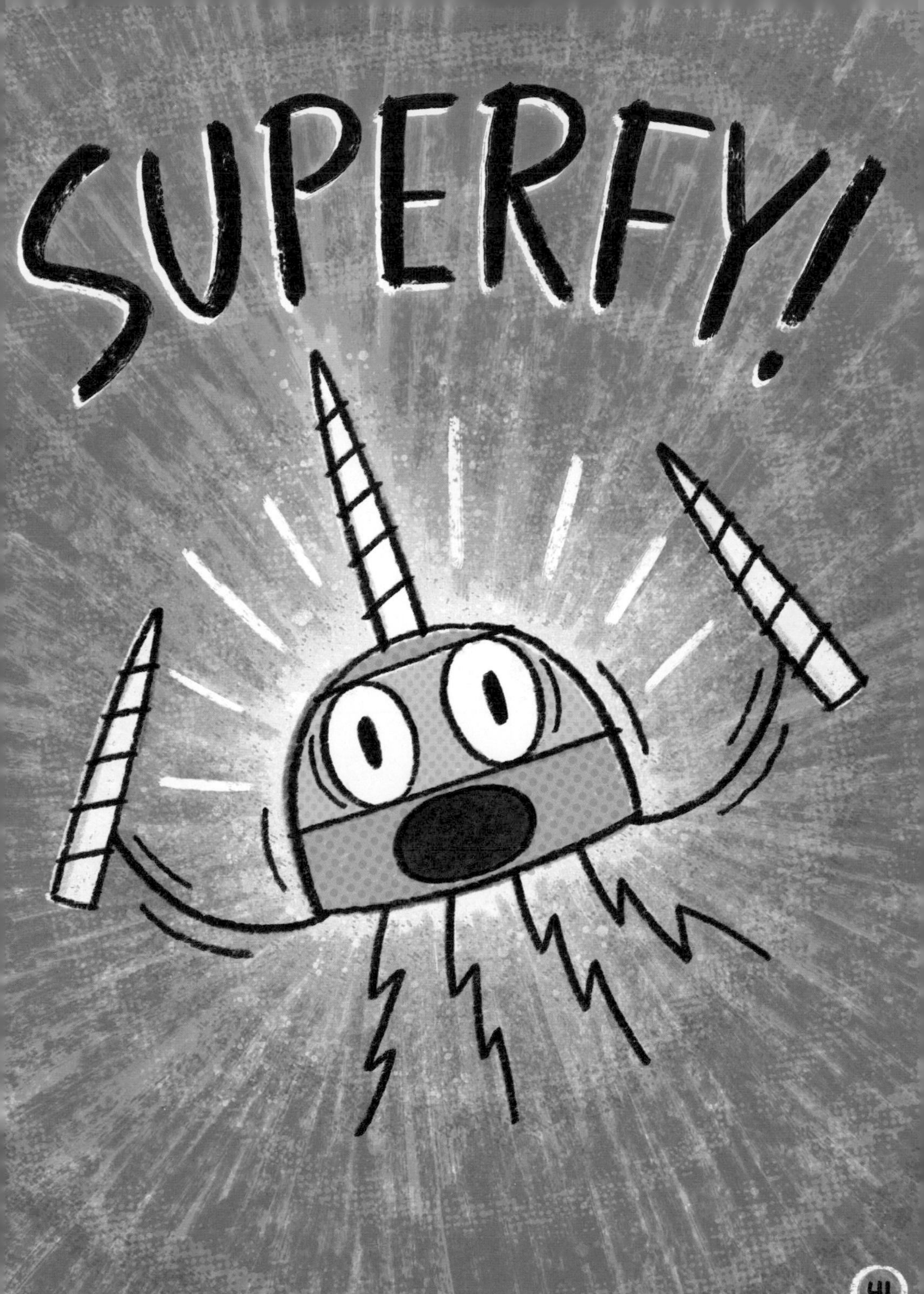
SUPERFLY!

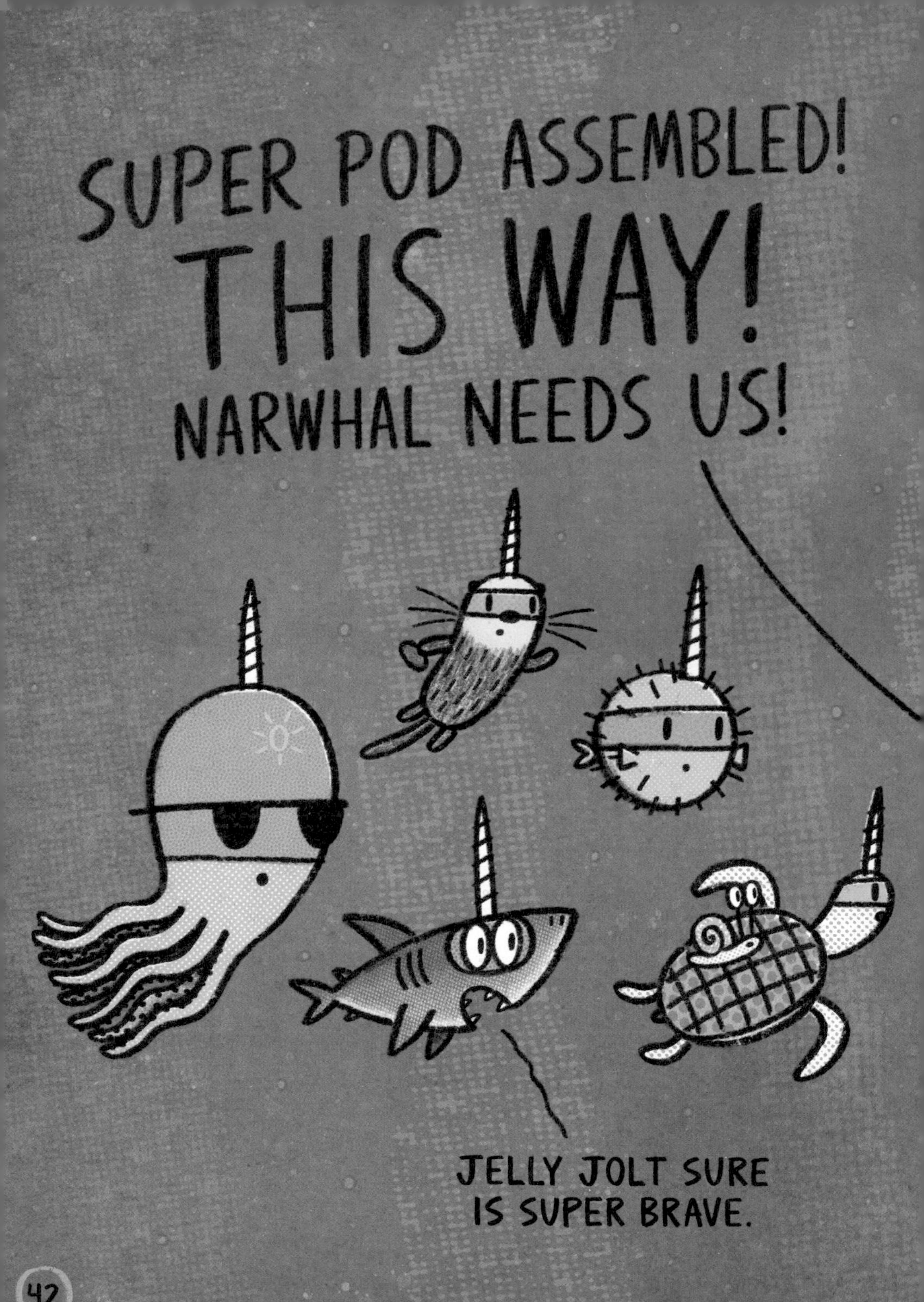

SUPER POD ASSEMBLED! THIS WAY! NARWHAL NEEDS US!
JELLY JOLT SURE IS SUPER BRAVE.

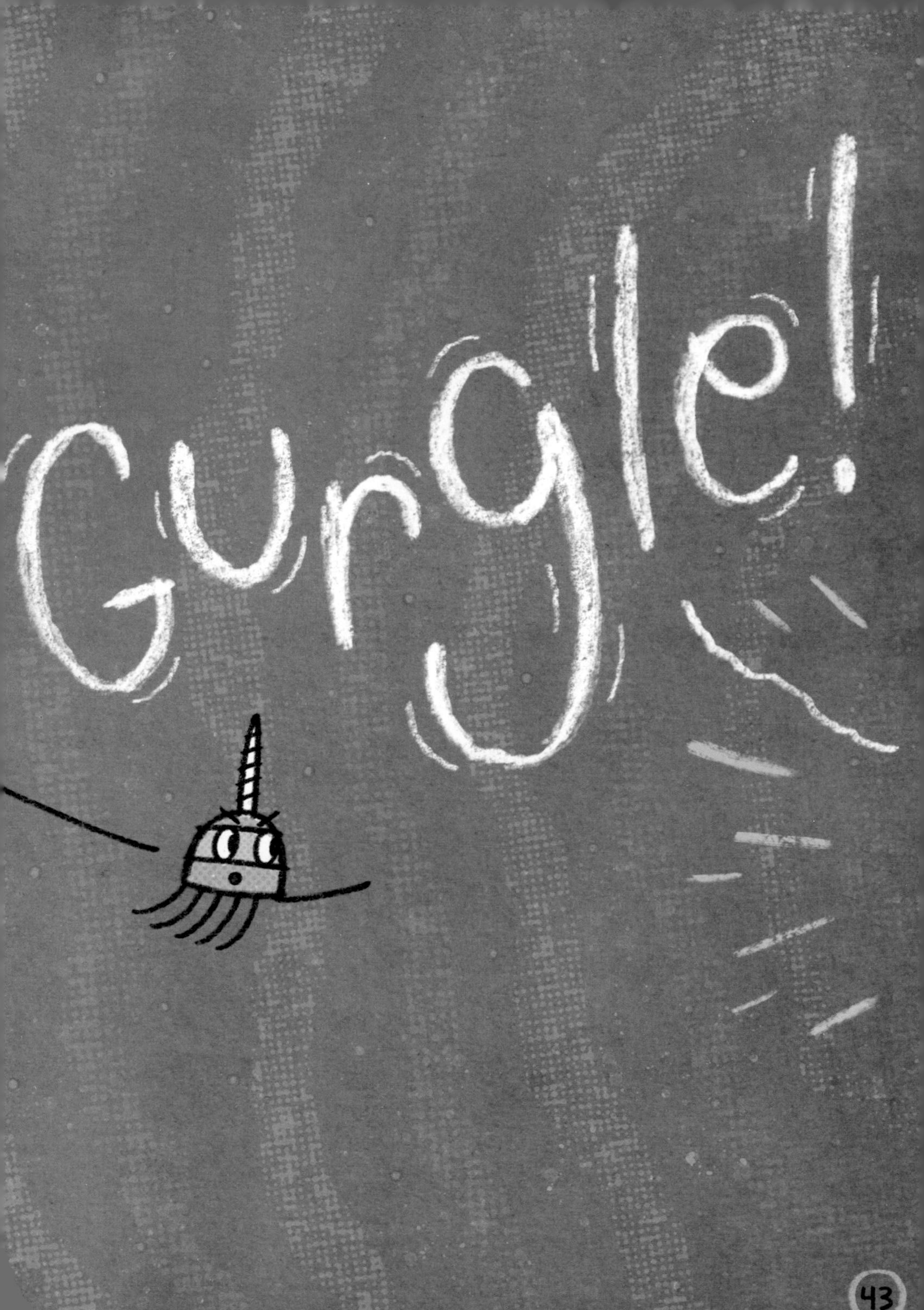
Gurgle!

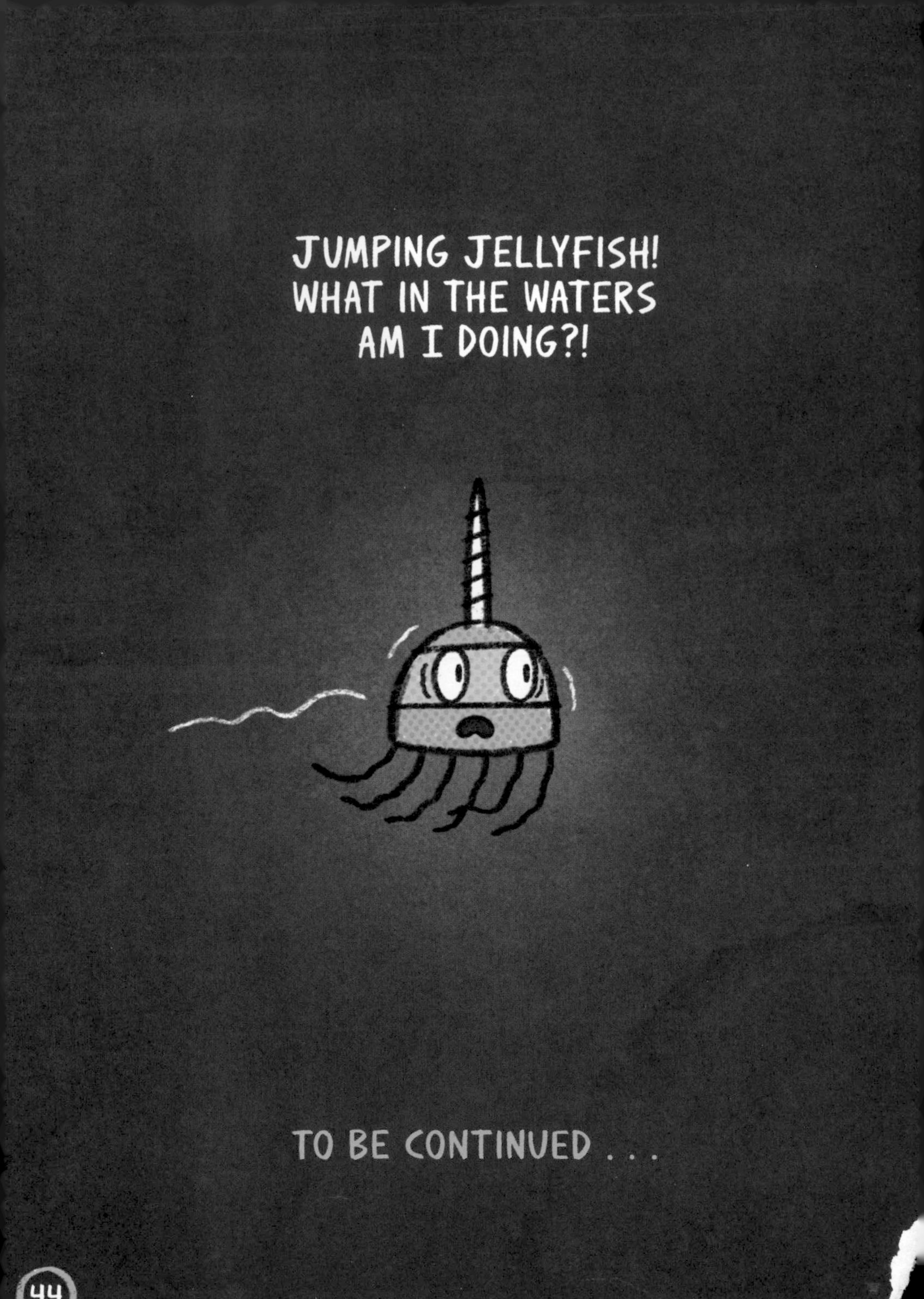
JUMPING JELLYFISH! WHAT IN THE WATERS AM I DOING?!
TO BE CONTINUED . . .

SUPER WAFFLE,
STRAWBERRY SIDEKICK
AND THE
BAT ATTACK

WAFFLE AND STRAWBERRY WERE JUST
ARRIVING AT PEAR'S HALLOWEEN PARTY
WHEN THEY HEARD . . .

EEK!

BAT!

ACK!

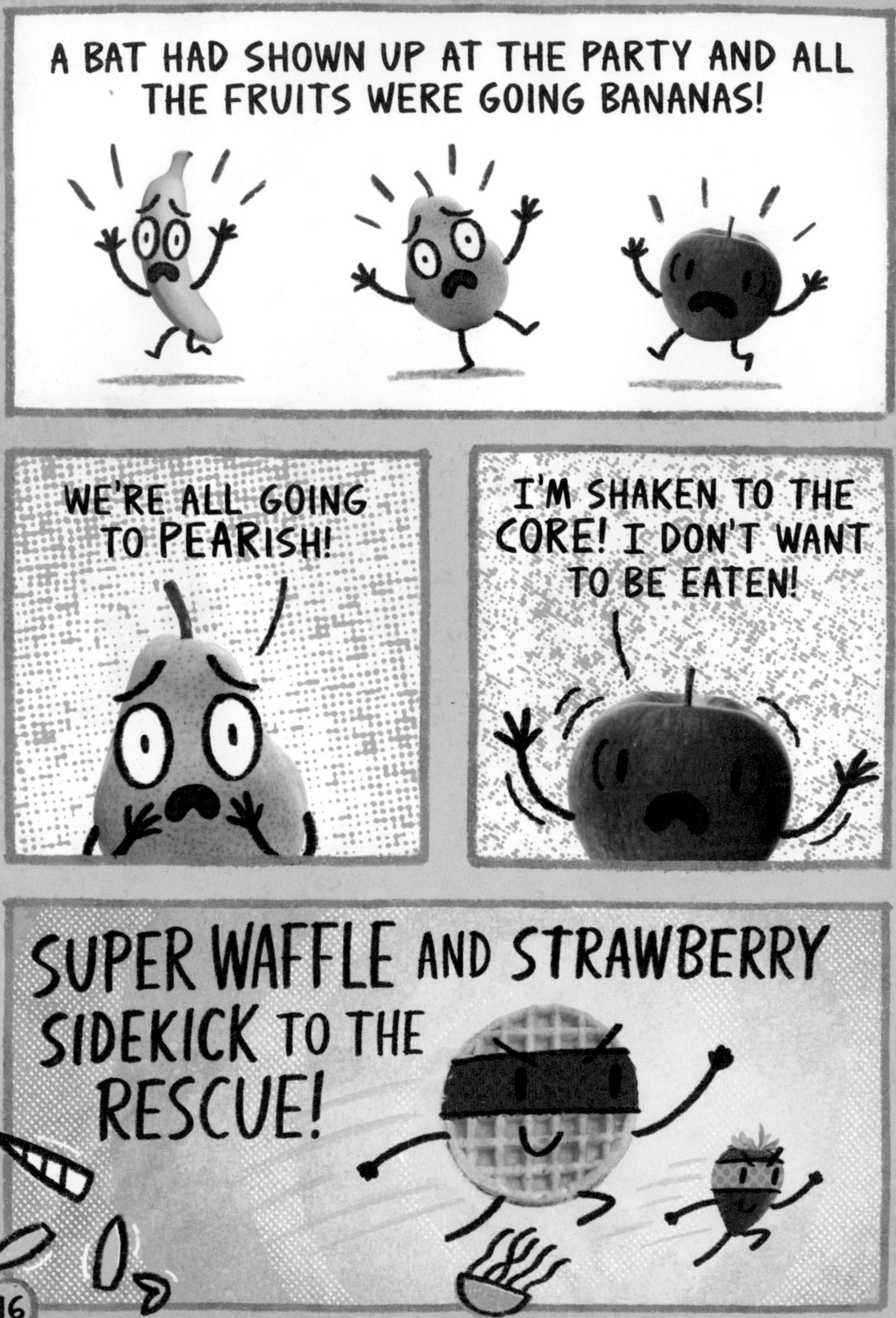
A BAT HAD SHOWN UP AT THE PARTY AND ALL THE FRUITS WERE GOING BANANAS!
WE'RE ALL GOING TO PEARISH!
I'M SHAKEN TO THE CORE! I DON'T WANT TO BE EATEN!
SUPER WAFFLE AND STRAWBERRY SIDEKICK TO THE RESCUE!

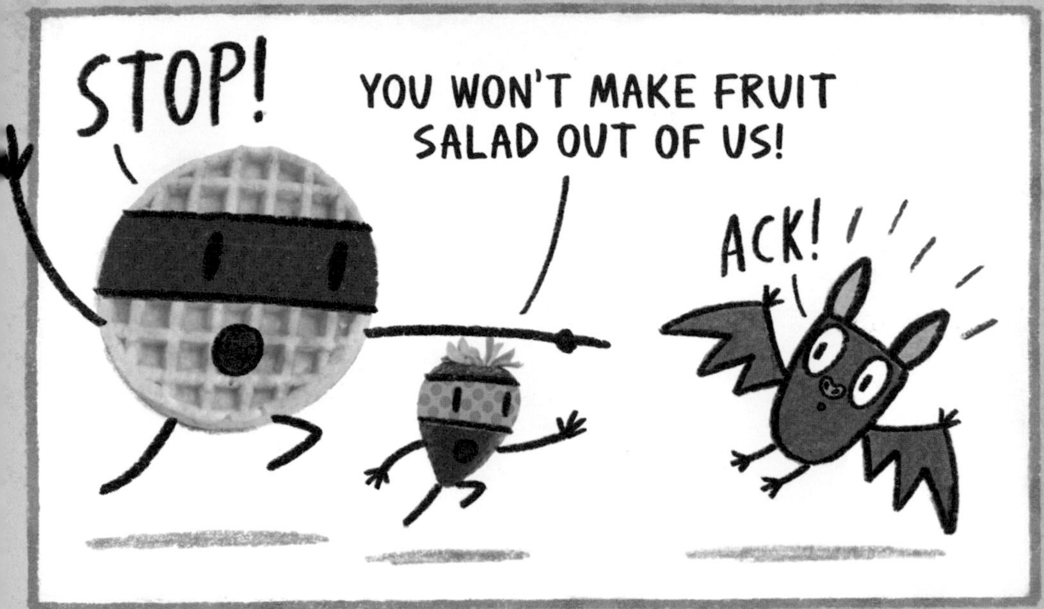
STOP!
YOU WON'T MAKE FRUIT SALAD OUT OF US!
ACK!

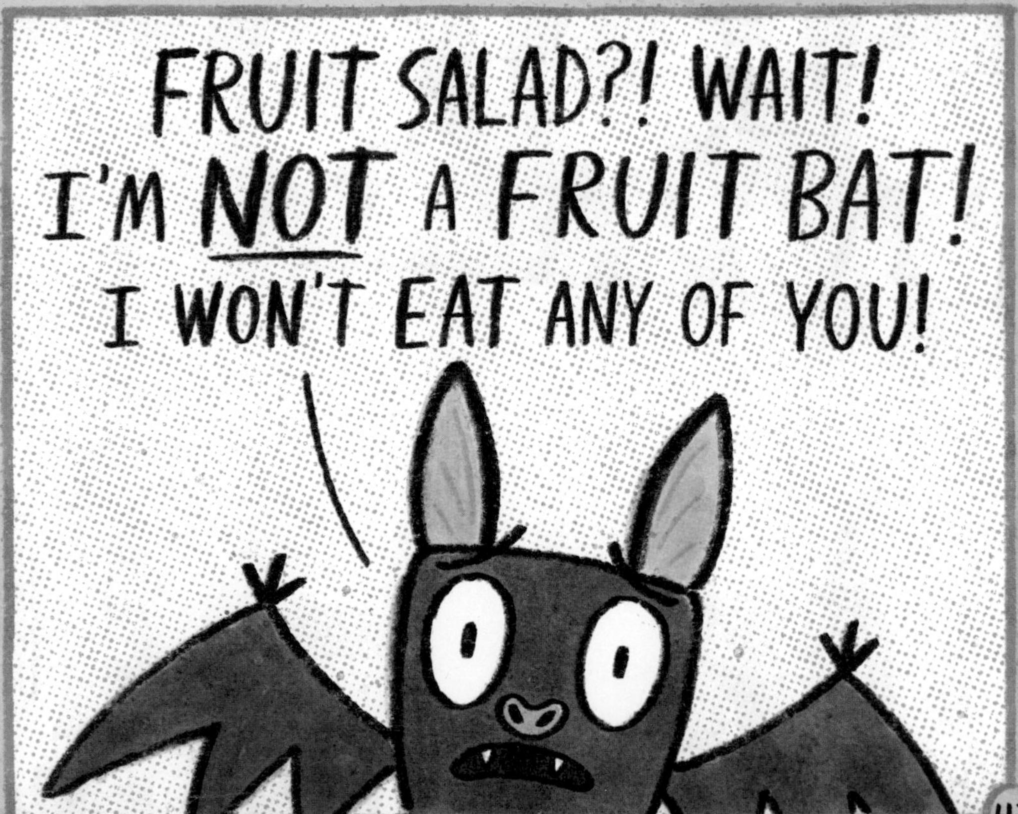
FRUIT SALAD?! WAIT! I'M NOT A FRUIT BAT! I WON'T EAT ANY OF YOU!

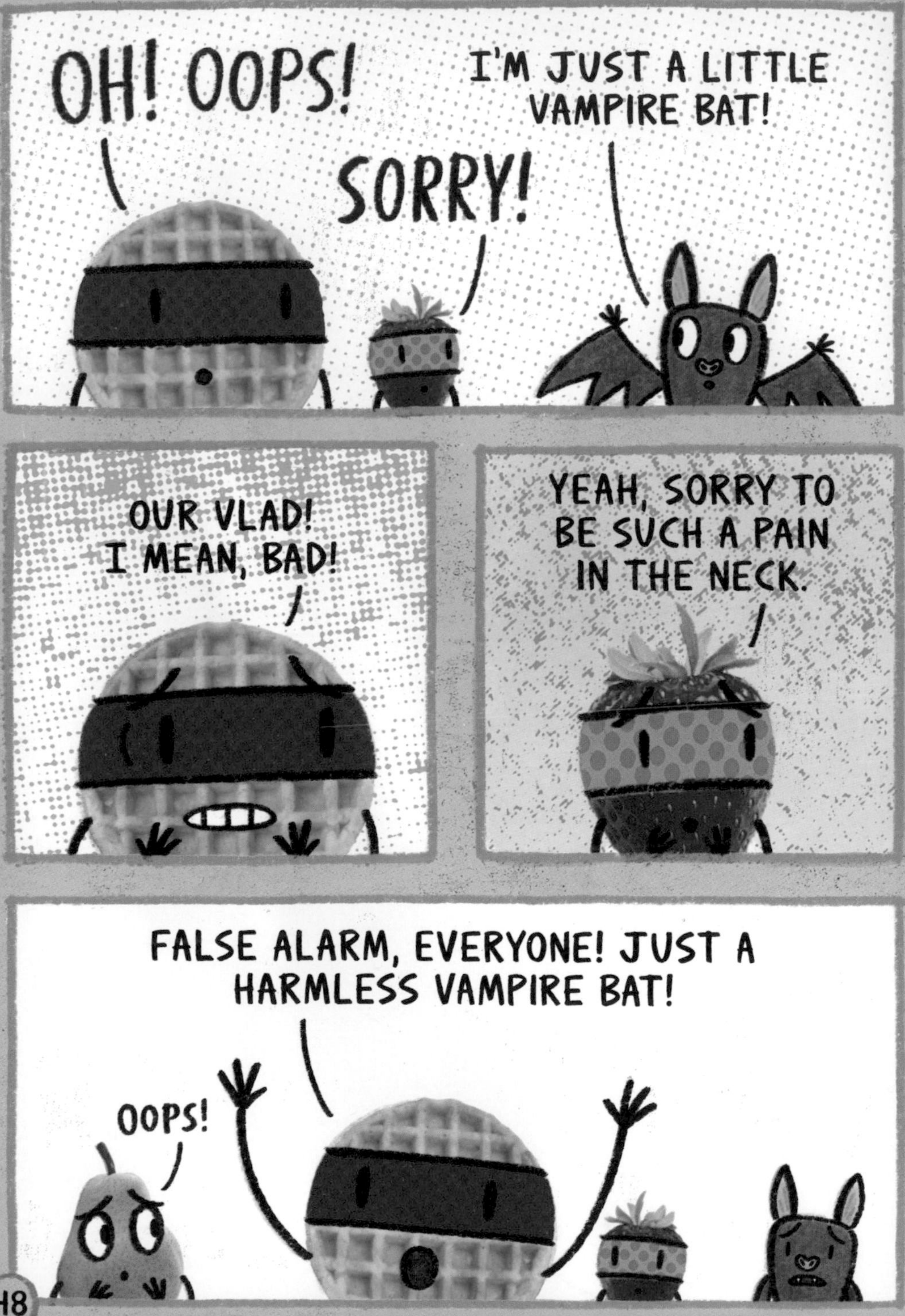

OH! OOPS!
SORRY!
I'M JUST A LITTLE VAMPIRE BAT!
OUR VLAD! I MEAN, BAD!
YEAH, SORRY TO BE SUCH A PAIN IN THE NECK.
FALSE ALARM, EVERYONE! JUST A HARMLESS VAMPIRE BAT!
OOPS!

ALL WAS FORGIVEN, AND WHAT FOLLOWED WAS THE MOST SUPER-AWESOME HALLOWEEN PARTY EVER.

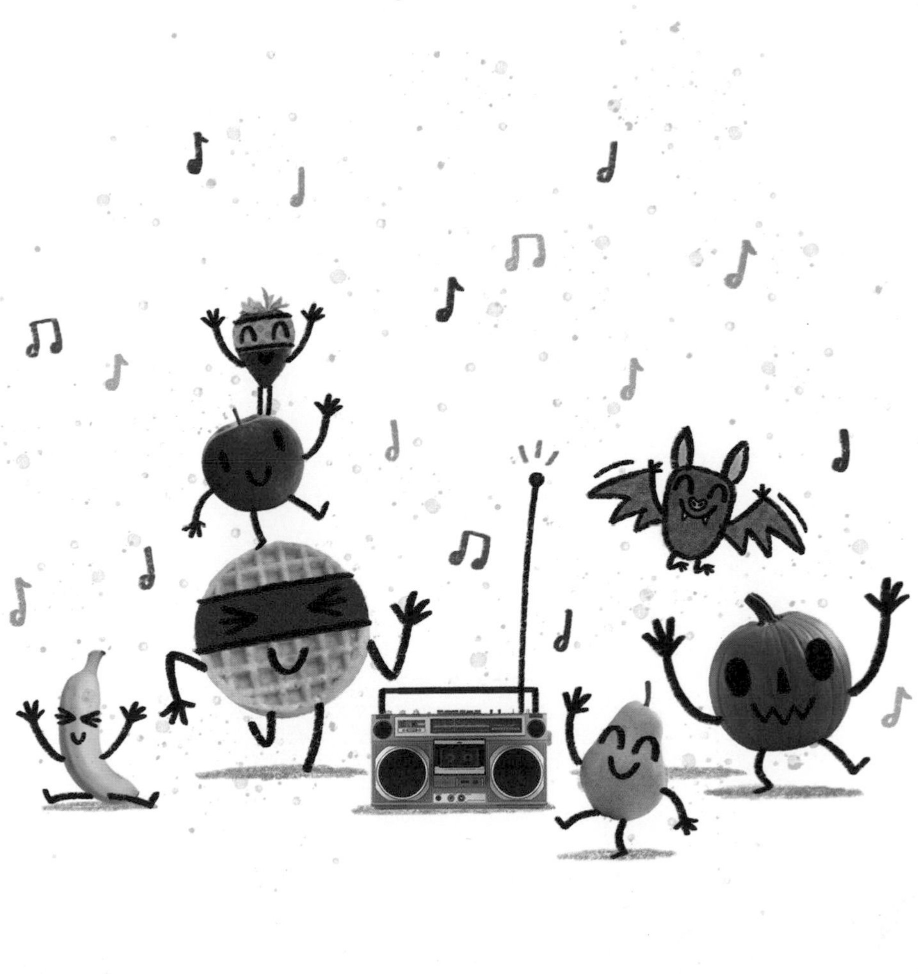

A BIT ABOUT BATS

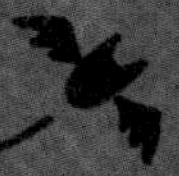

THERE ARE OVER 1,400 KINDS (SPECIES) OF BATS IN THE WORLD, RANGING FROM FRUIT BATS TO VAMPIRE BATS TO ITTY-BITTY BUMBLEBEE BATS.

WOW!

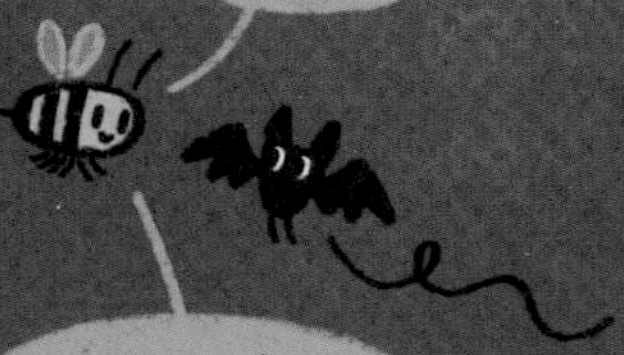

I CAN'T BEELIEVE IT! A BAT AS BIG AS ME!

HUH! I'M STARTING TO HAVE A GOOD PEELING ABOUT BATS!

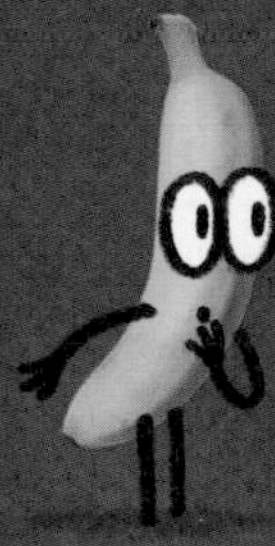

BATS PLAY AN IMPORTANT ROLE FOR OVER 300 SPECIES OF FRUIT – THEY HELP POLLINATE BANANAS, AVOCADOS AND MANGOES.

THAT'S POOPER! I MEAN, SUPER!

BAT DROPPINGS, ALSO KNOWN AS GUANO, ARE A RICH FERTILIZER!

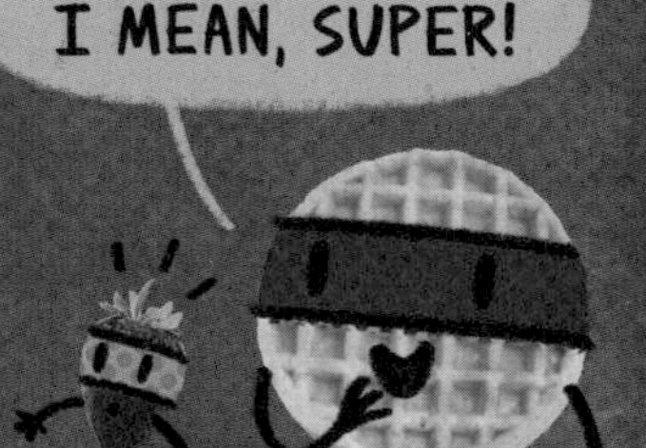

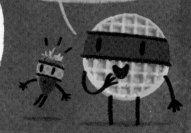

JELLY JOLT

AND THE

MONSTROUS
MESS!

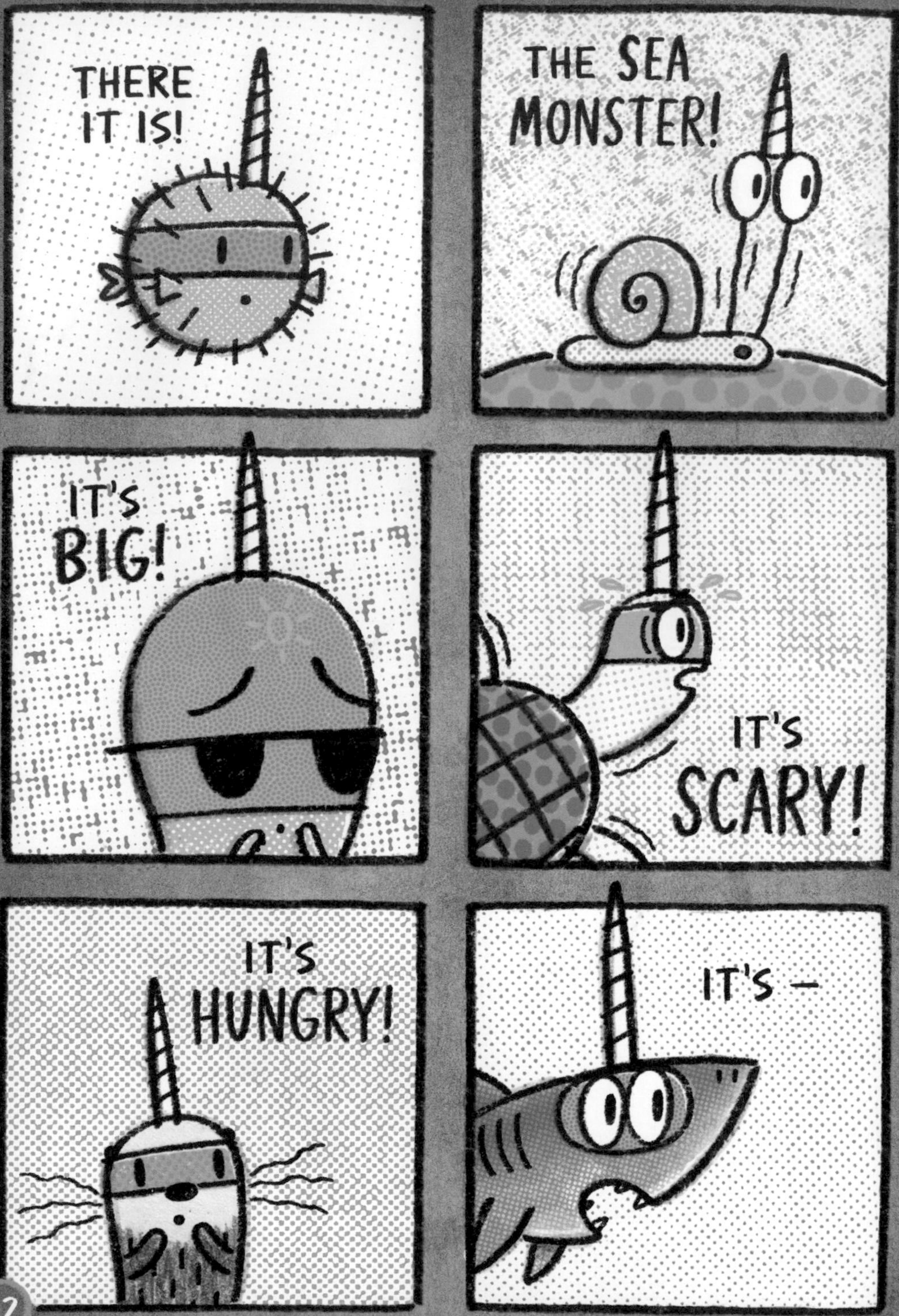
THERE IT IS!
THE SEA MONSTER!
IT'S BIG!
IT'S SCARY!
IT'S HUNGRY!
IT'S —

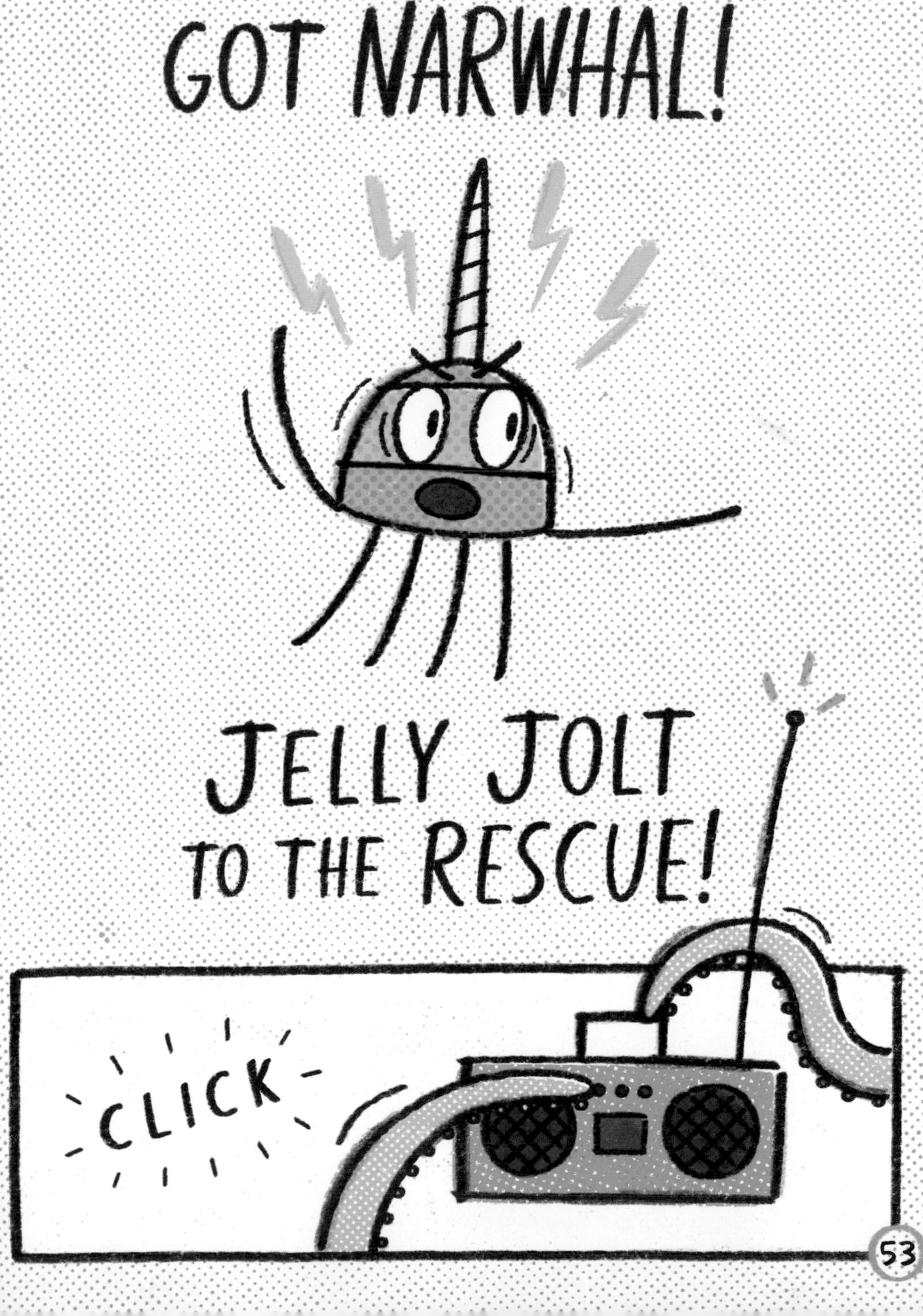
GOT NARWHAL!
JELLY JOLT TO THE RESCUE!
CLICK

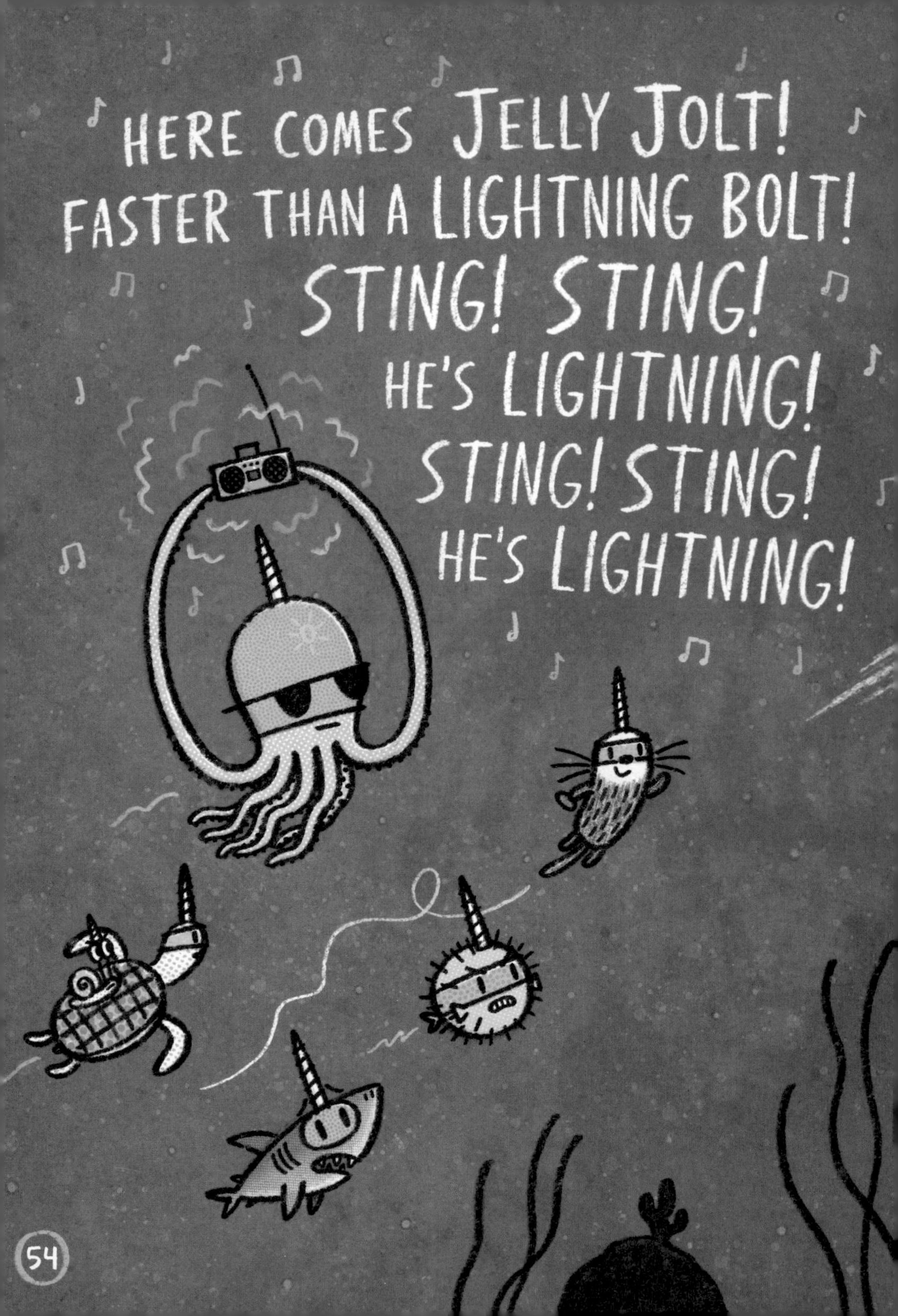
HERE COMES JELLY JOLT!
FASTER THAN A LIGHTNING BOLT!
STING! STING!
HE'S LIGHTNING!
STING! STING!
HE'S LIGHTNING!

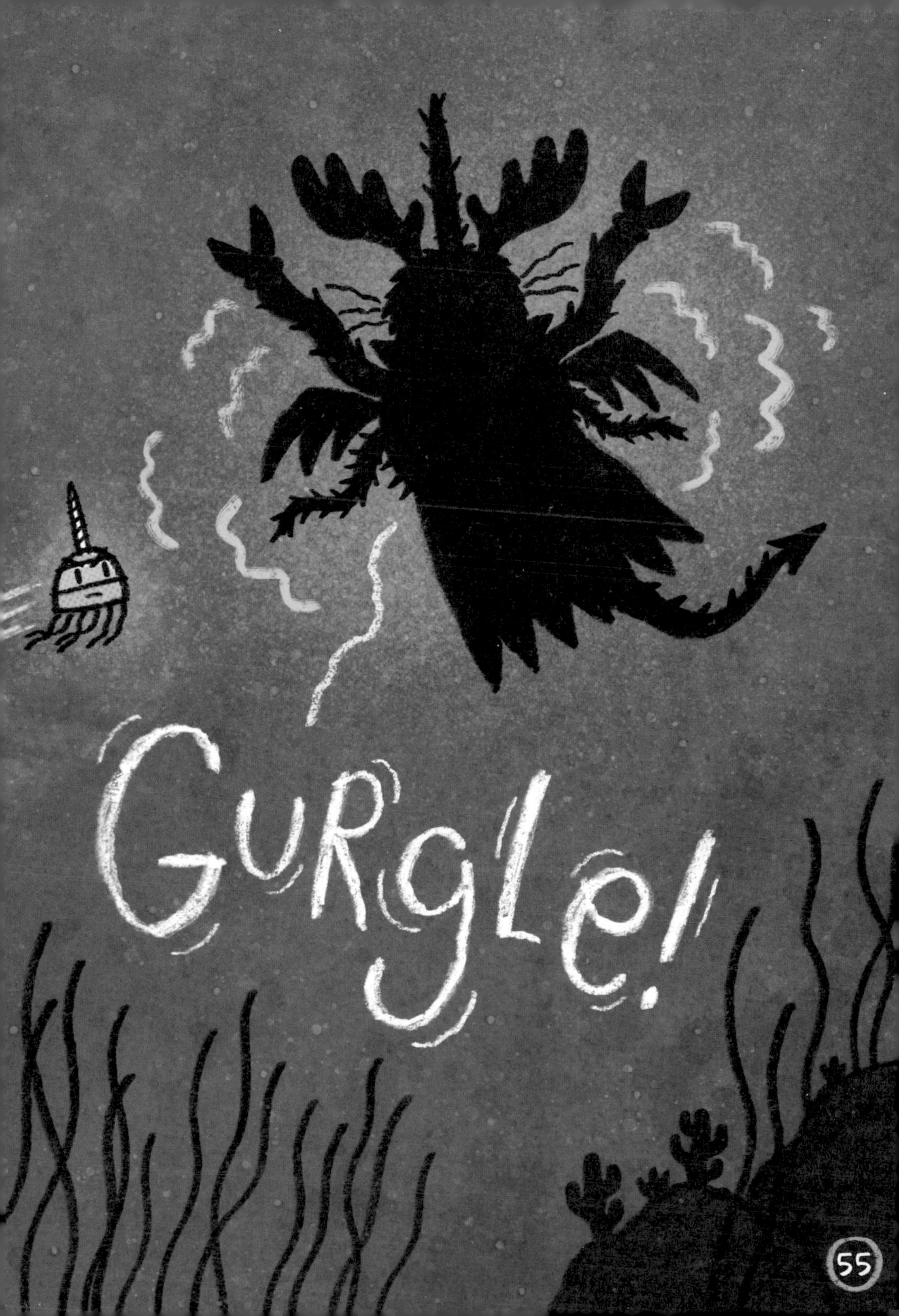
GURGLE!

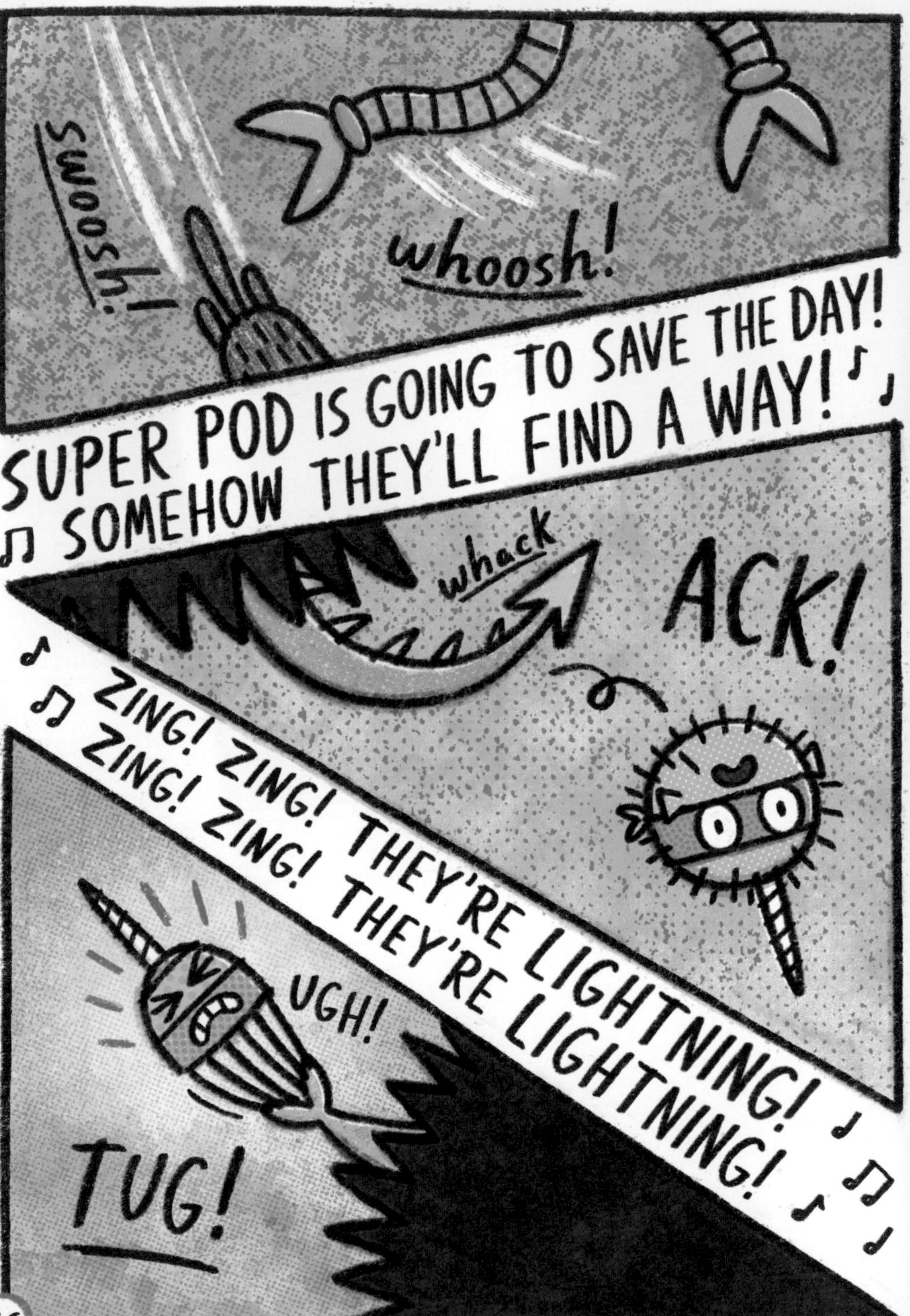
swoosh!
whoosh!
SUPER POD IS GOING TO SAVE THE DAY!
♫ SOMEHOW THEY'LL FIND A WAY! ♪
whack
ACK!
♪ ZING! ZING! THEY'RE LIGHTNING!
♫ ZING! ZING! THEY'RE LIGHTNING! ♫
UGH!
TUG!

(INSERT EPIC GUITAR SOLO)

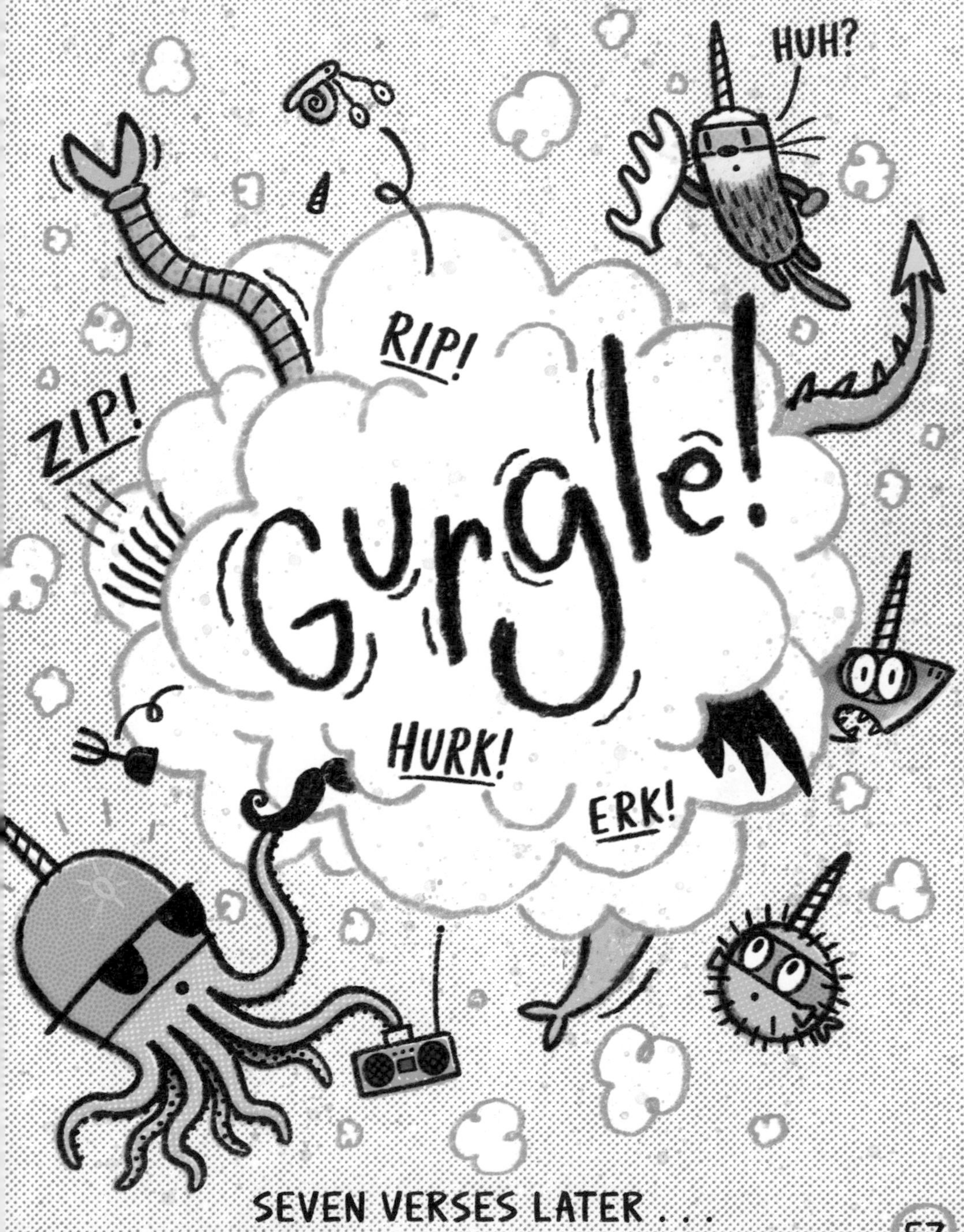
HUH?
RIP!
ZIP!
Gurgle!
HURK!
ERK!

SEVEN VERSES LATER . . .

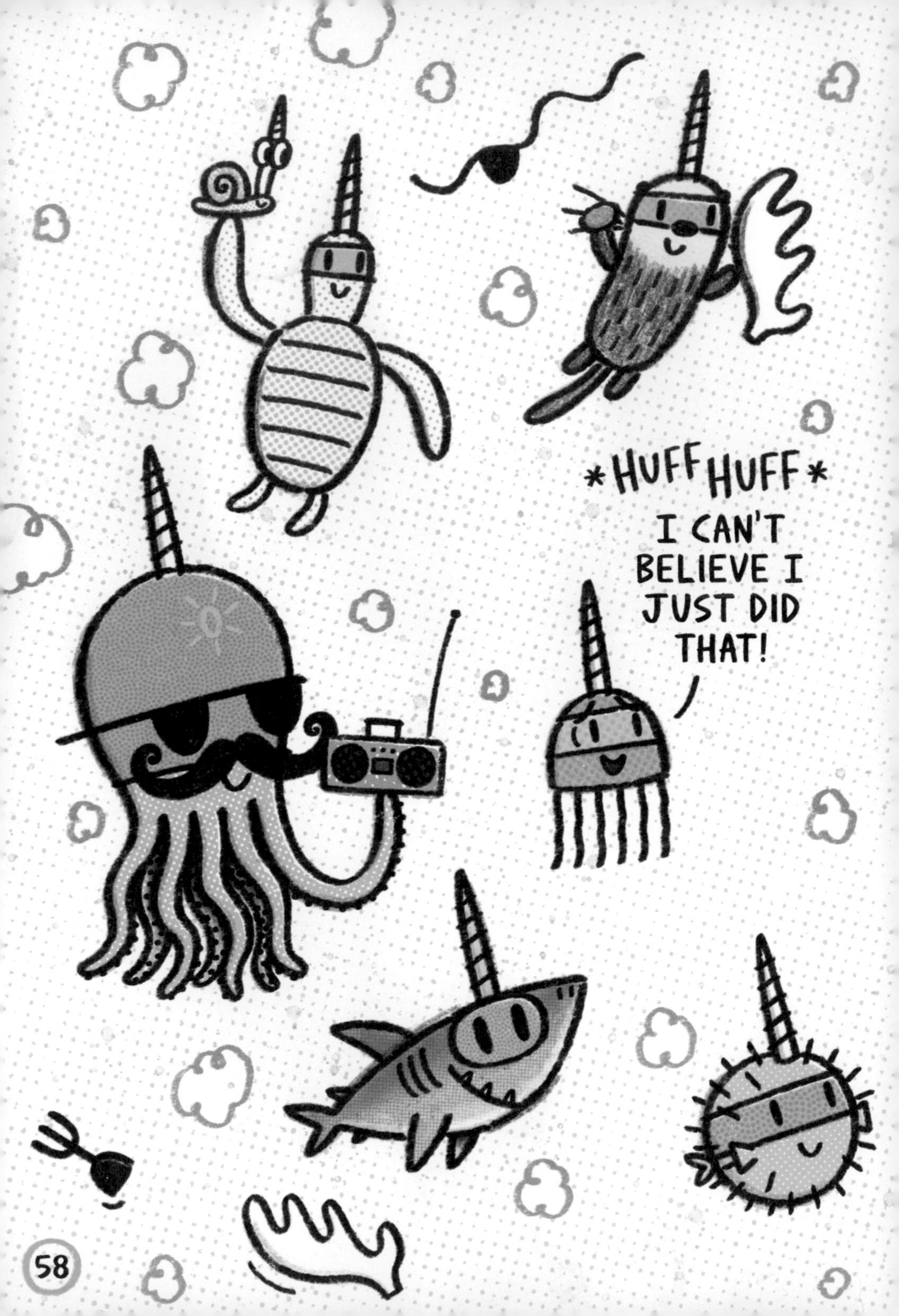
HUFF HUFF
I CAN'T BELIEVE I JUST DID THAT!

JELLY JOLT!
YOU SAVED ME!

THANK YOU ALL
FOR BEING
SUCH SUPER
PODSOME PALS!

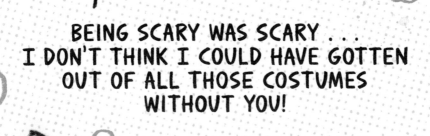

BEING SCARY WAS SCARY . . .
I DON'T THINK I COULD HAVE GOTTEN
OUT OF ALL THOSE COSTUMES
WITHOUT YOU!

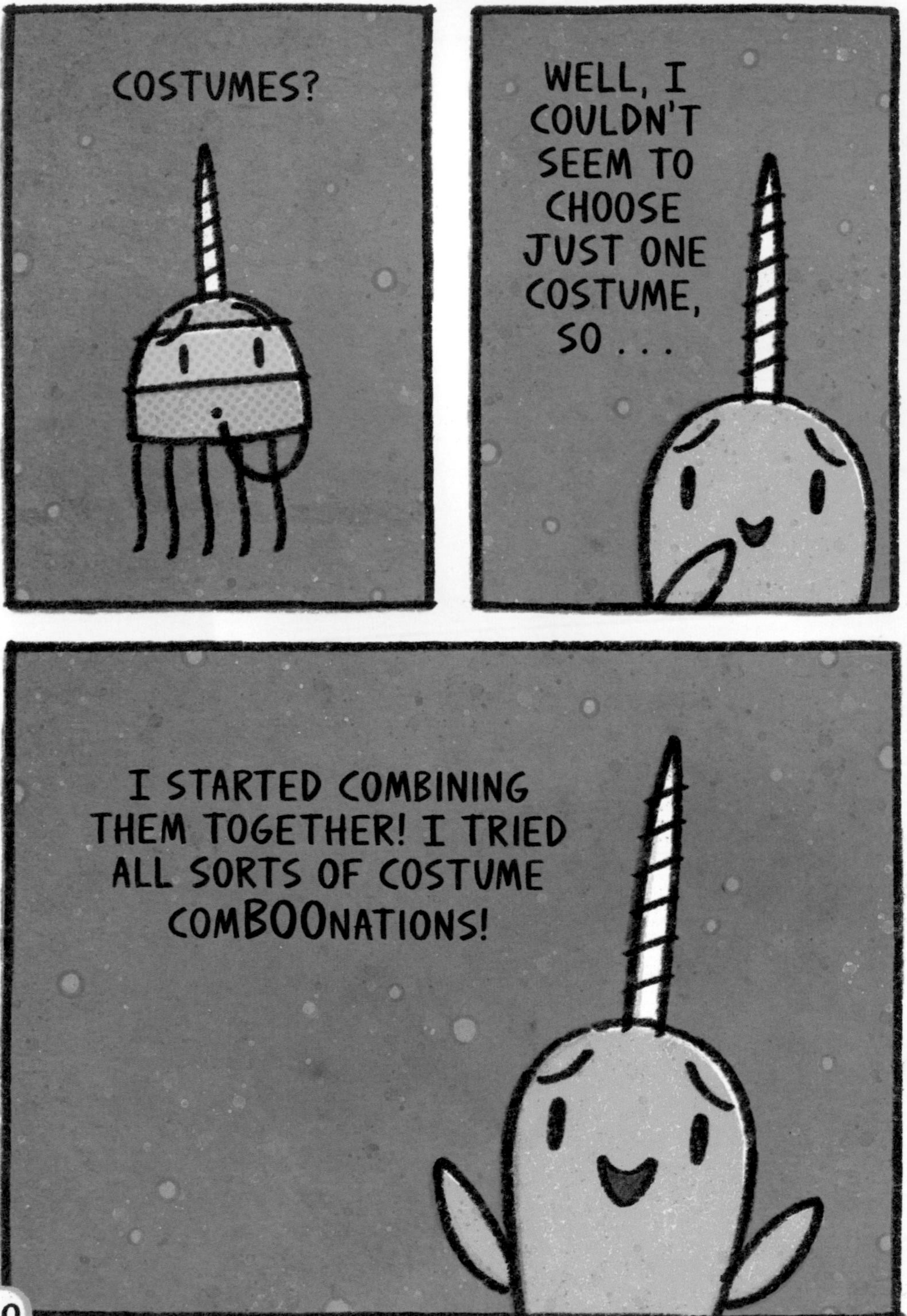
COSTUMES?
WELL, I COULDN'T SEEM TO CHOOSE JUST ONE COSTUME, SO . . .
I STARTED COMBINING THEM TOGETHER! I TRIED ALL SORTS OF COSTUME COMBOONATIONS!

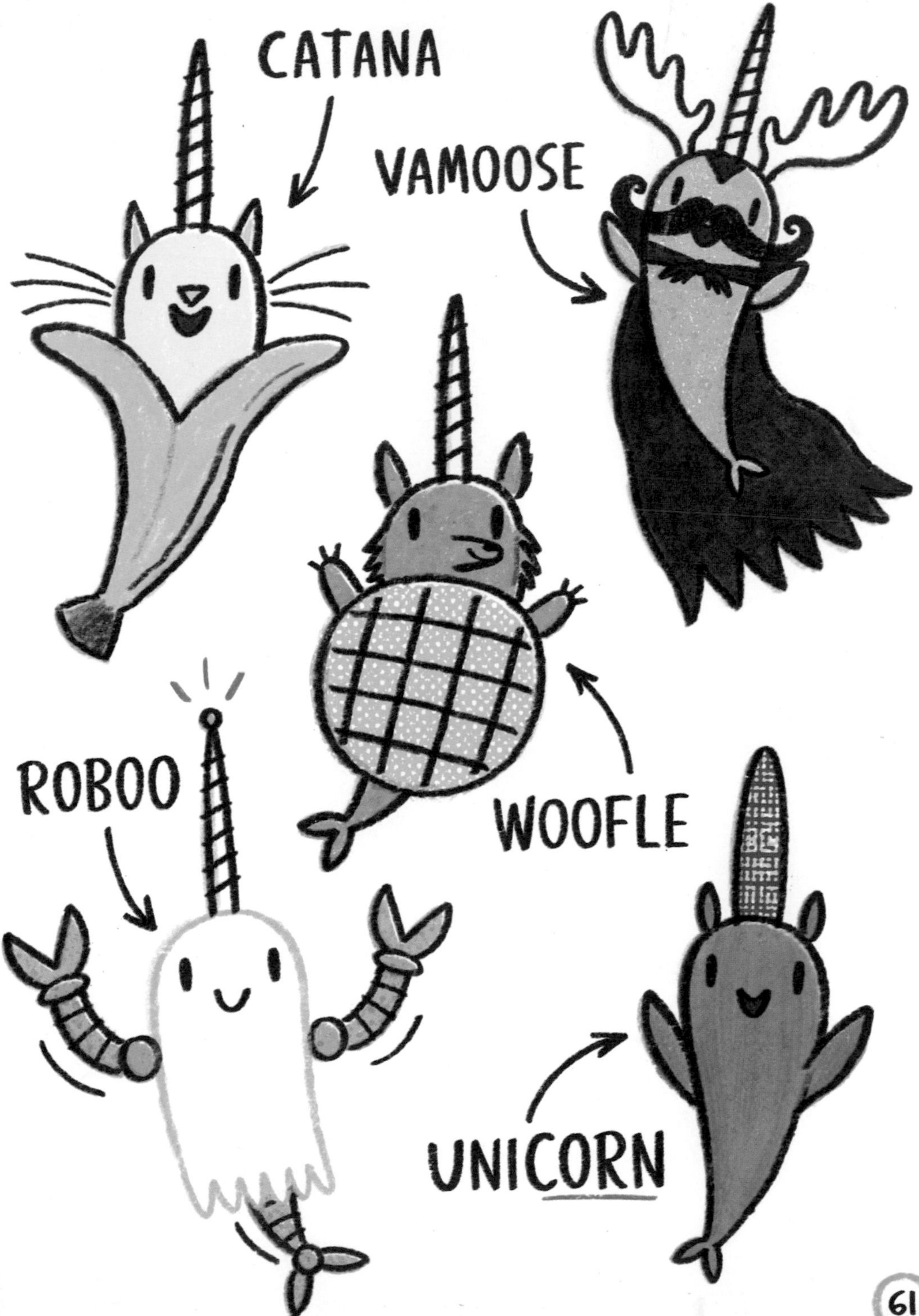
CATANA
VAMOOSE
WOOFLE
ROBOO
UNICORN

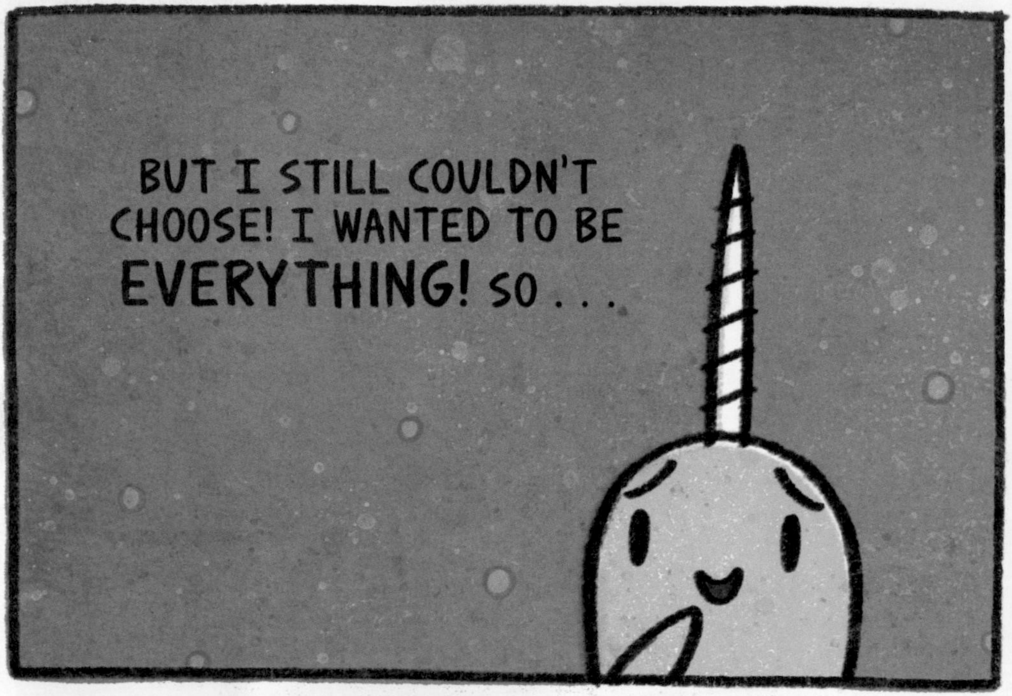
BUT I STILL COULDN'T CHOOSE! I WANTED TO BE EVERYTHING! SO . . .

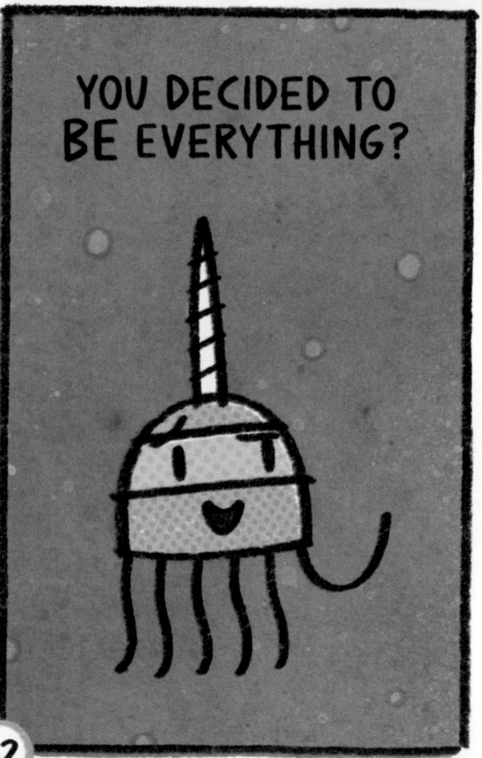
YOU DECIDED TO BE EVERYTHING?

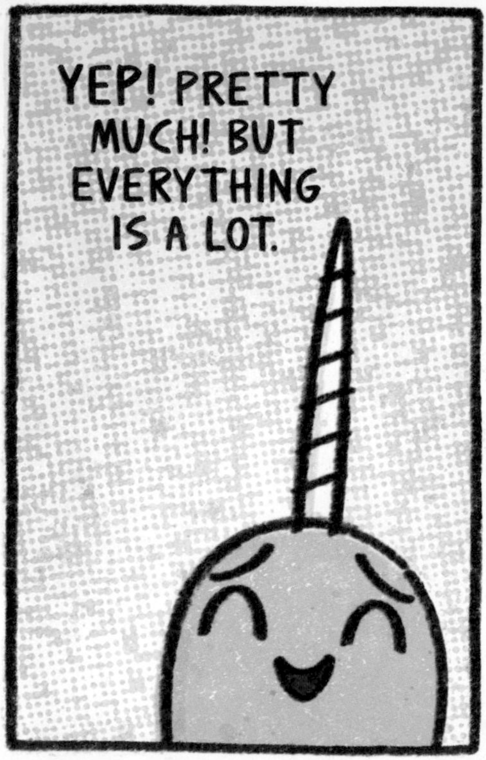
YEP! PRETTY MUCH! BUT EVERYTHING IS A LOT.

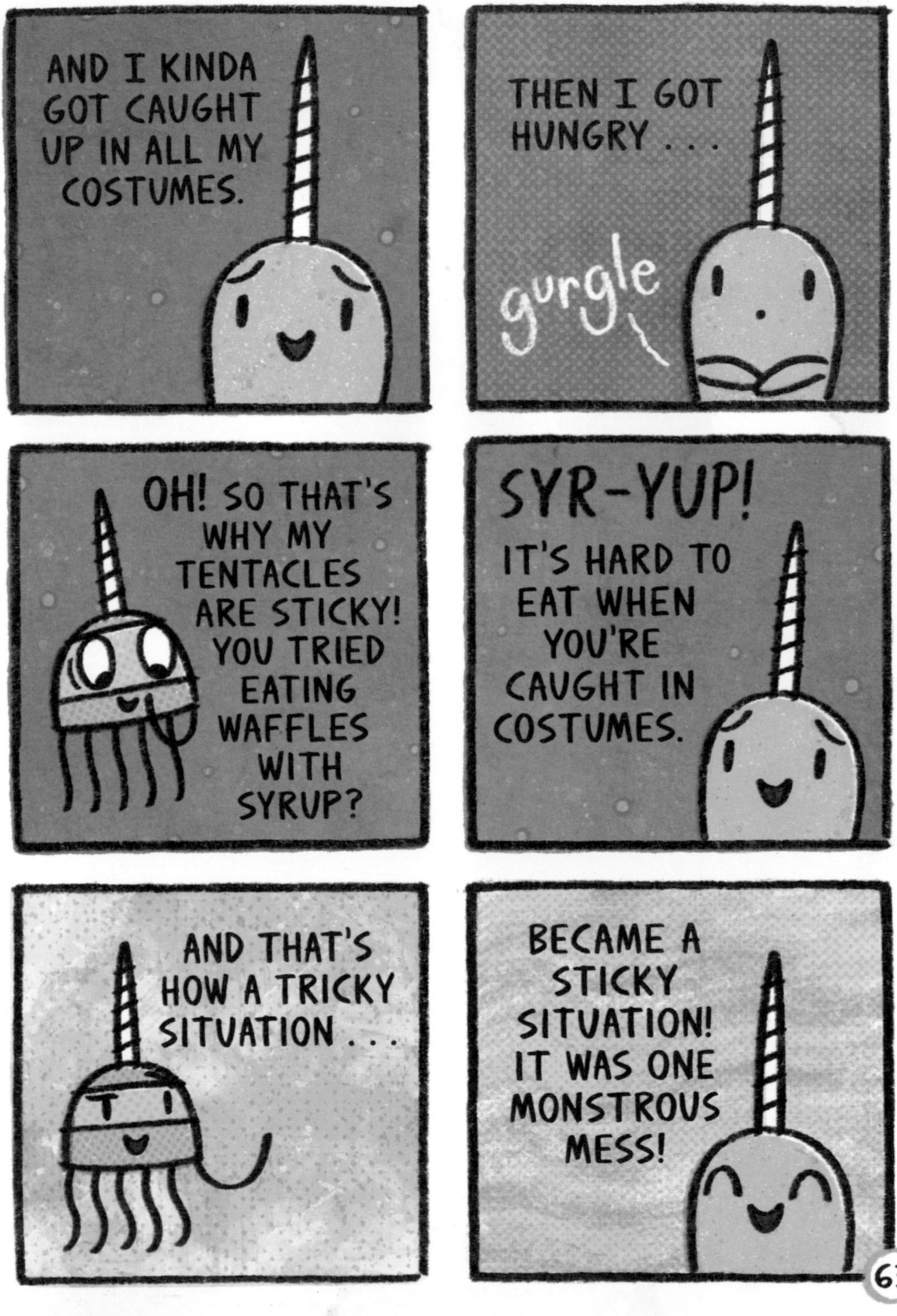
AND I KINDA GOT CAUGHT UP IN ALL MY COSTUMES.
THEN I GOT HUNGRY . . .
gurgle
OH! SO THAT'S WHY MY TENTACLES ARE STICKY! YOU TRIED EATING WAFFLES WITH SYRUP?
SYR-YUP!
IT'S HARD TO EAT WHEN YOU'RE CAUGHT IN COSTUMES.
AND THAT'S HOW A TRICKY SITUATION . . .
BECAME A STICKY SITUATION! IT WAS ONE MONSTROUS MESS!

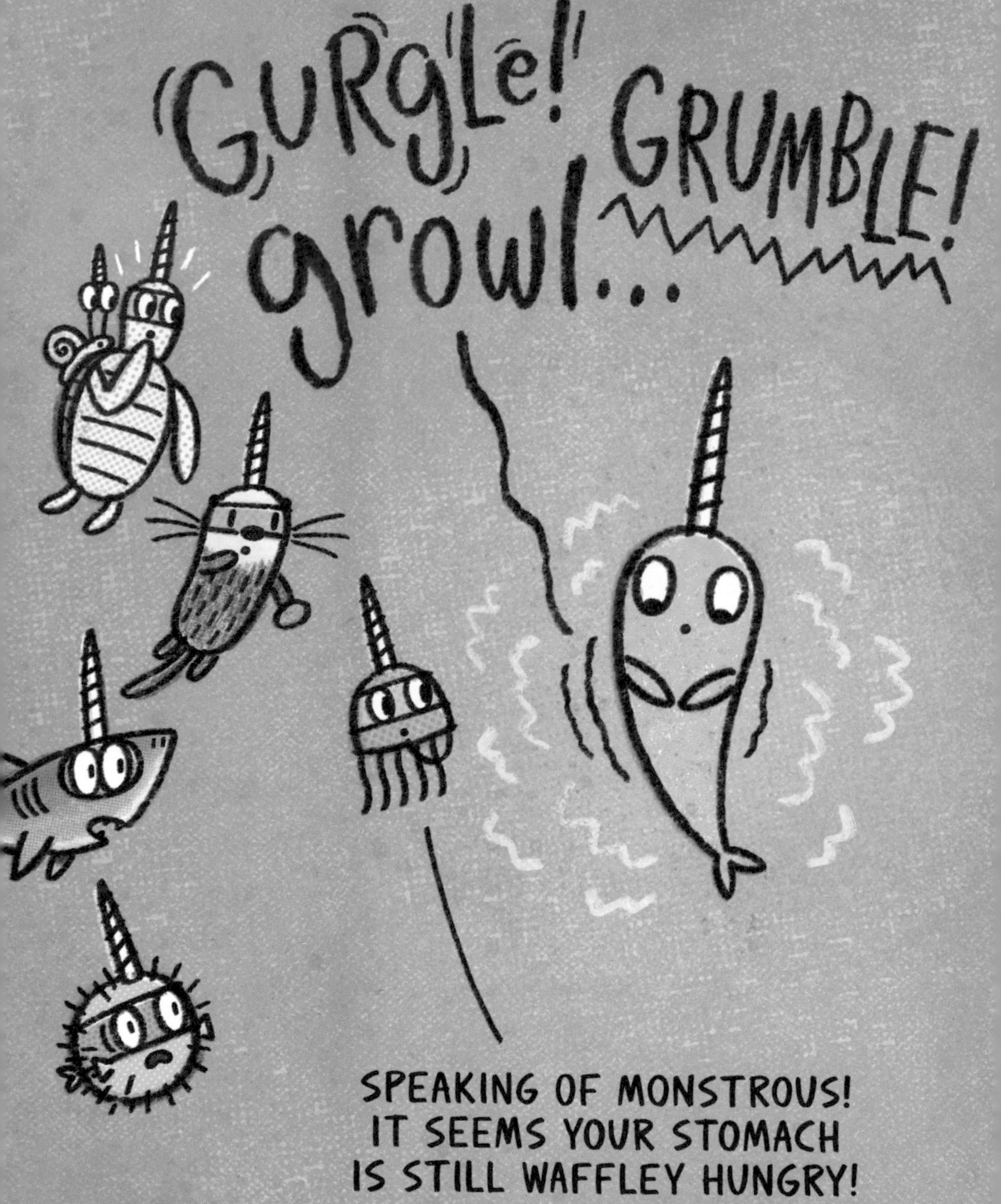
GURGLE!
GRUMBLE!
growl...
SPEAKING OF MONSTROUS!
IT SEEMS YOUR STOMACH
IS STILL WAFFLEY HUNGRY!

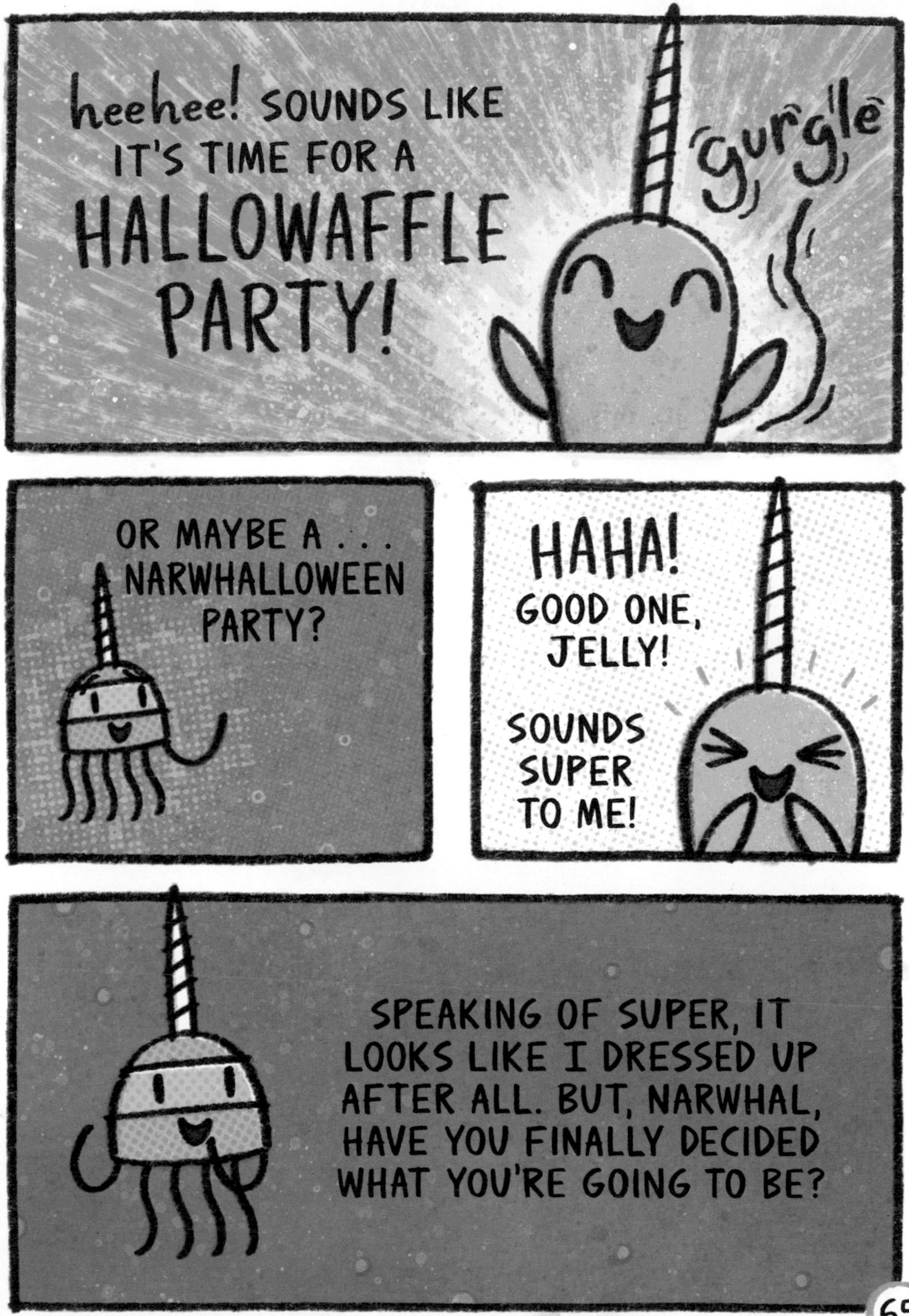
heehee! SOUNDS LIKE IT'S TIME FOR A HALLOWAFFLE PARTY!
gurgle
OR MAYBE A . . . NARWHALLOWEEN PARTY?
HAHA! GOOD ONE, JELLY!
SOUNDS SUPER TO ME!
SPEAKING OF SUPER, IT LOOKS LIKE I DRESSED UP AFTER ALL. BUT, NARWHAL, HAVE YOU FINALLY DECIDED WHAT YOU'RE GOING TO BE?

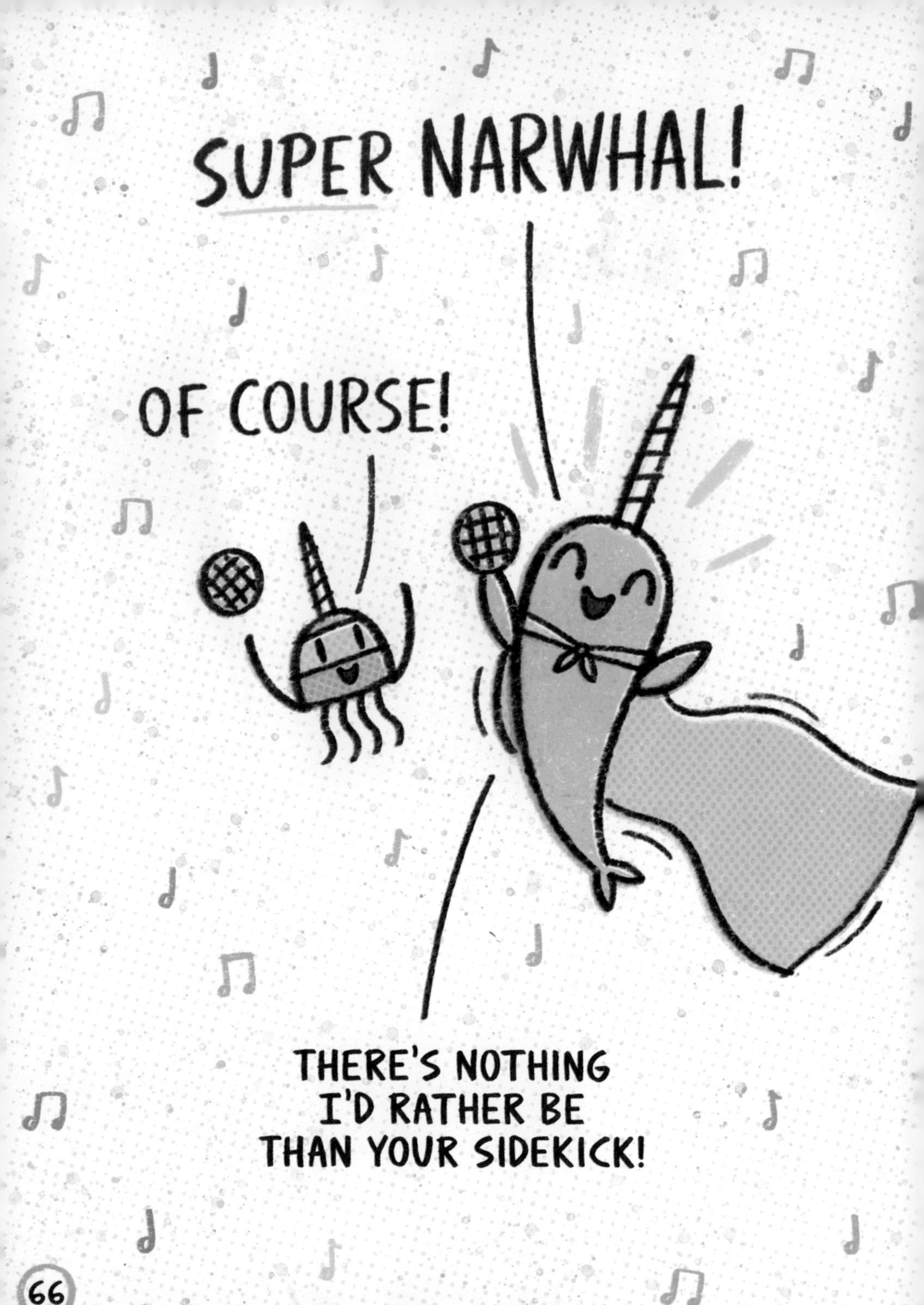
SUPER NARWHAL!
OF COURSE!
THERE'S NOTHING I'D RATHER BE THAN YOUR SIDEKICK!

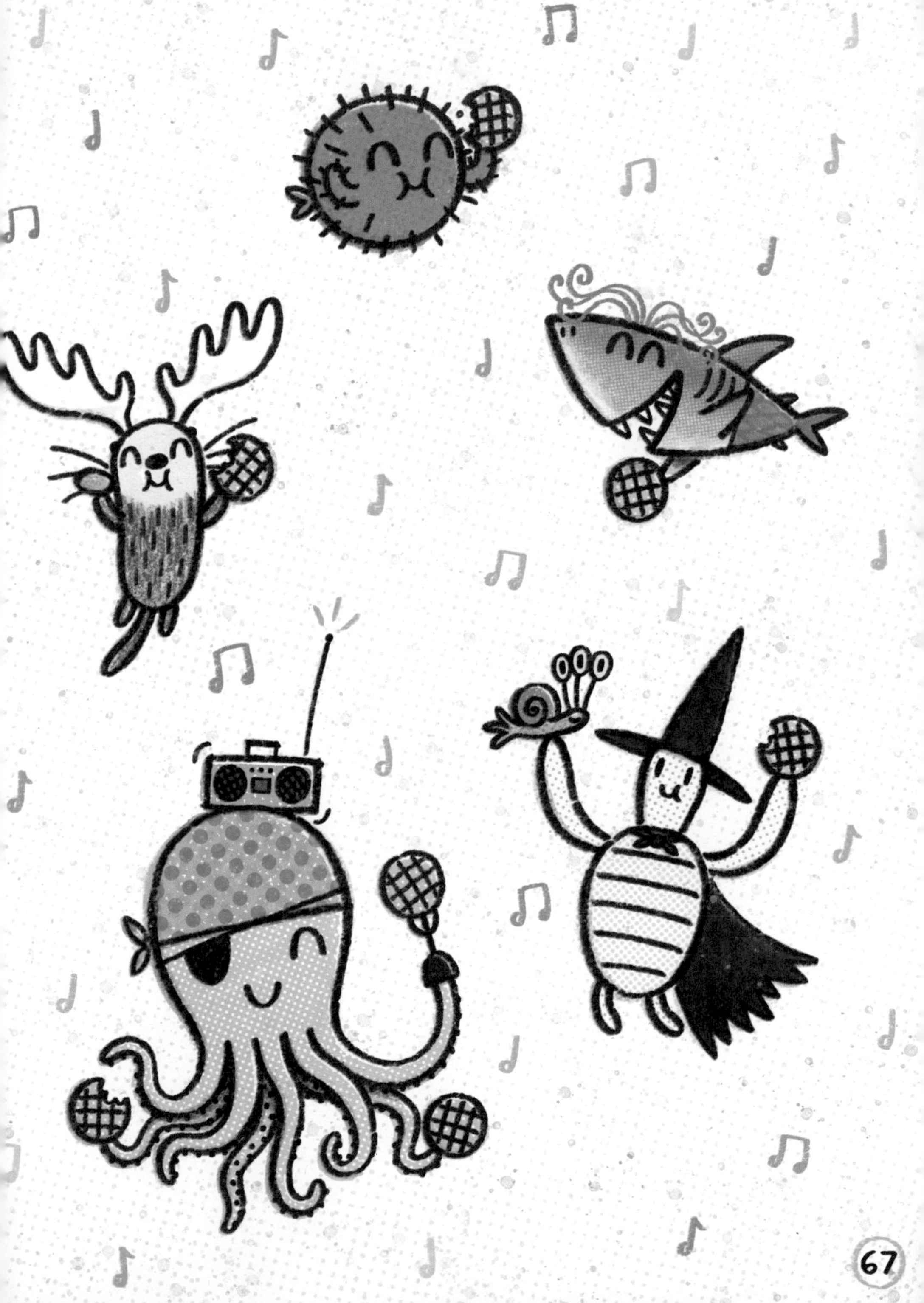

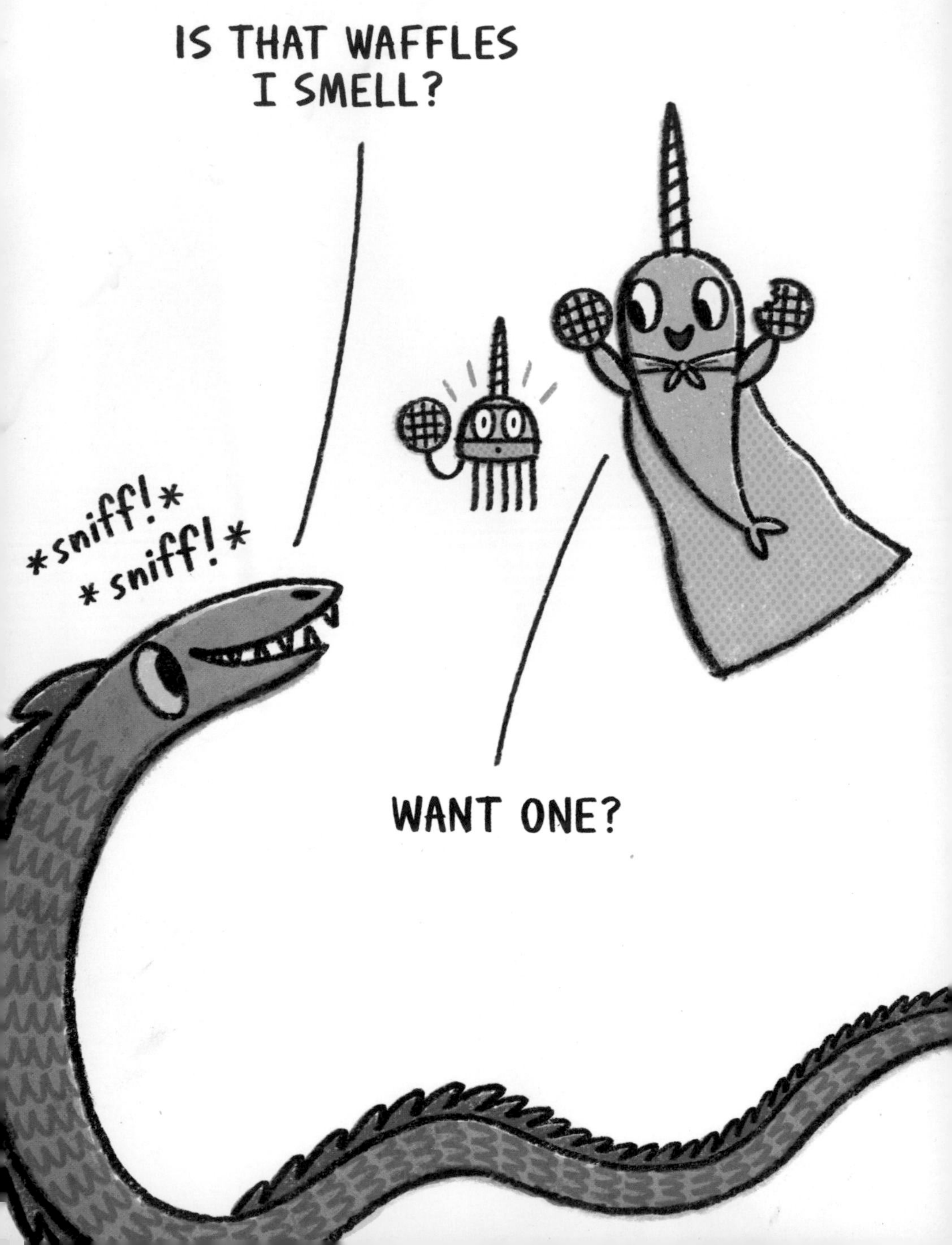
IS THAT WAFFLES I SMELL?
sniff!
sniff!
WANT ONE?

HAPPY NARWHALLOWEEN!

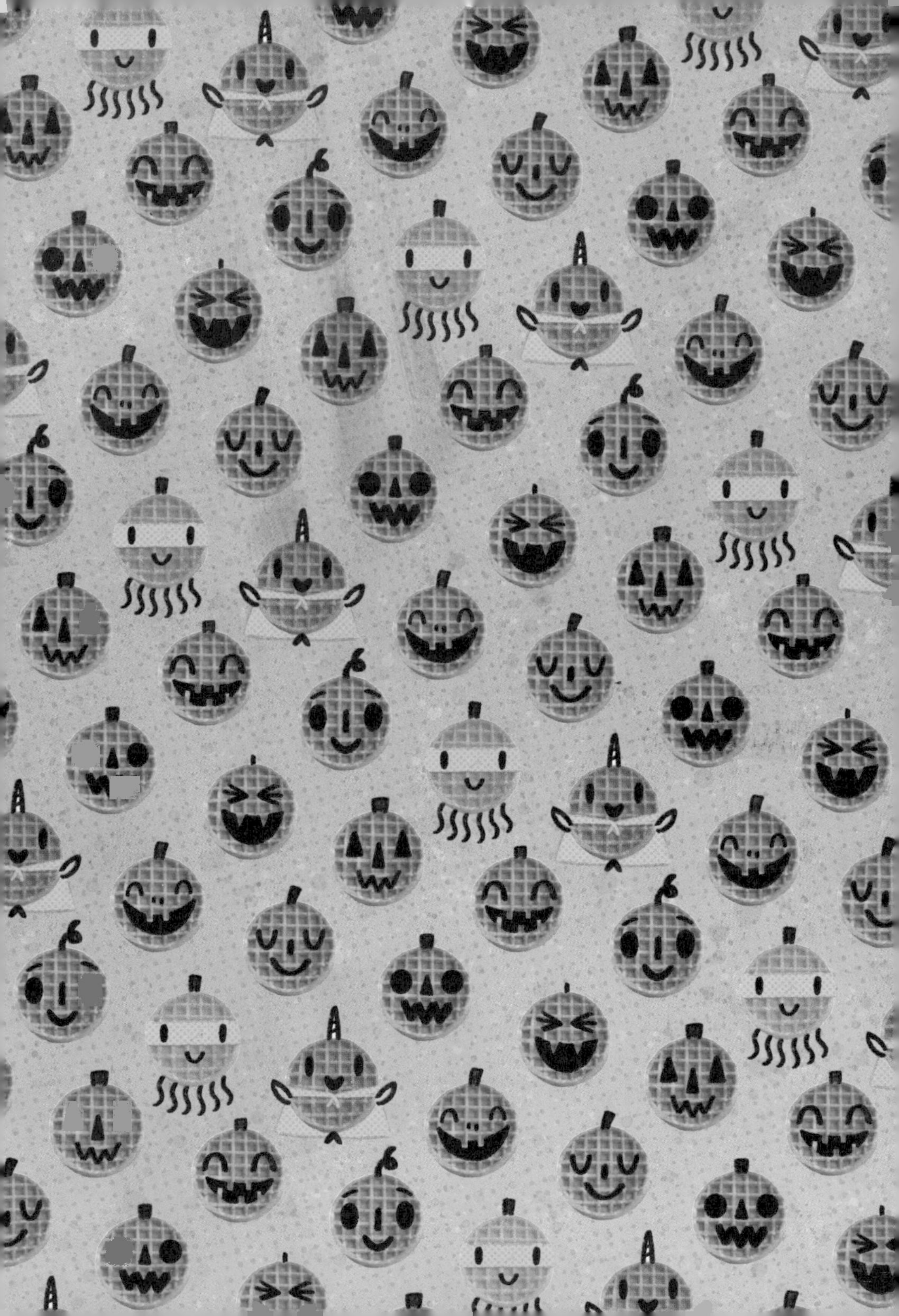